COPYRIGHT

DEDICATION

To Jae Ashley: Thank you for your hard work and patience throughout this project.

CHAPTER 1

THE FIRST thing I hated about him was his smile. Nobody genuinely smiles that much. It's fake. I don't trust fake people; they tend to hide things. And Korban Keller was as fake as they came.

He was older than me. Not by much, just a few years. With our packs being relatively close in proximity, I had seen him a handful of times when we were boys.

My clearest memory of him back then was of his eyes—they were a rich navy, the color of the deepest part of the ocean. He had a weird habit of tracking me with those eyes, and I wondered if it was because he planned to attack me or if he was waiting to catch me making a mistake so he could call me out on it in front of everybody. Whatever the reason, it distracted me, so when we were in the same room, I struggled to focus on anything other than Korban watching me.

His father was Alpha of the Miancarem pack, which lived on the edge of the same forest as my pack, Yafenack. But where their pack lands started on the northern end of the forest and abutted a human town, ours began in the center and continued with dense woods protected by a wide spring on one end and a rocky mountain on the other. The humans built a highway on the other side of the creek, but it didn't have an exit near our town, so we remained secluded and safe.

Even at age eight, I understood the Yafenack pack would be my responsibility one day. I needed to learn how to be a good Alpha, so I rarely left my father's side. Korban was in line to be Alpha of his pack too, but he seemed to have no sense of duty.

My first time going to an interpack council meeting with my father, Korban walked right up to me and said, "Hi."

It was weird.

After thinking about the best way to respond to the son of the Miancarem Alpha and eliminating a couple of options, I finally went with, "Hello."

"I'm Korban Keller." He smiled so broadly his nose crinkled a little. "What's your name?"

I glanced up at my father to see if he could help me figure out how to deal with the unexpected interrogation, but he was busy talking with the other adults.

"I'm Samuel Goodwin," I said eventually.

"How old are you, Sam?"

I hated being called Sam. I also hated being asked questions when I didn't know why they were being asked. And I didn't like people poking their noses in my business. But on the other hand, I worried it'd be considered rude if I didn't answer. I'd have to work with this boy one day because I'd be Alpha of my pack, he'd be Alpha of his pack, and my father said getting along with people was important. I wasn't sure why or if I agreed, but he was a smart man and I tried to listen to him.

"I'm eight."

"Cool. I'm eleven."

He kept grinning and looking at me. I wondered if I was supposed to say something or if we were done talking and he'd go away so I could stop feeling nervous and focus on my dad's conversation.

"You want to go play, Sam?"

"It's Samuel!" I snapped.

His eyes widened in surprise, but that was his only reaction to my obvious annoyance. "Do you want to go play, Samuel?"

I looked him over and tried to figure out what he was doing.

"They have a football in the back."

I stared at him.

"And the yard is really big."

Big as in big enough that nobody would hear me if I got hurt? Was he threatening me?

"But if you don't like football, they have checkers too."

Why wouldn't I be able to play football? I was one of the strongest boys in my grade and, yes, Korban was bigger than me, but that was only because he was older.

"If you like checkers." He smiled again, but it wasn't as big that time. There was something softer about it. "It's okay if you don't."

Oh, so now I wasn't strong enough for football and I wasn't smart enough for checkers. The nerve of that guy!

"We can shift instead. I bet we can find good stuff to sniff when we're in our wolf forms."

The conversation made me uncomfortable. He made me uncomfortable. I felt off-balance and confused, which was probably exactly what he intended. No way was I wandering off with him away from my father and the other adults. No way.

"I don't think I'm supposed to—"

"Go ahead, Samuel," my father said.

Surprised he was listening to our conversation, I jerked my gaze up.

"I'm sure you'd much rather play outside with your new friend than stand in here listening to a bunch of boring old guys talk." He winked at me, smiled, and then ruffled my hair as he said, "Go on."

I growled a little, not happy about this turn of events. Why would my father send me off with someone who made me feel strange? It was probably more of his training about getting along well with others. He was constantly talking to me about that and asking who I hung out with at school and why I didn't have friends over to the house.

"Fine," I grunted. "We can shift."

Football was okay. Checkers too. But I was stronger in my wolf form, always had been. It was easier to follow my instincts as a wolf, and I wasn't hampered by the constant questions I had in my human form about what I was supposed to say or do, neither of which came naturally to me.

"Great!" Korban grabbed my hand and yanked me toward the door. "Let's go."

Shocked that he was touching me, I could only follow speechlessly while my mind reeled. Wolves were naturally affectionate, I knew that. When our pack members shifted, cubs often rolled together on the ground and adults nipped at each other playfully. But that was different. They were friends or family members. And besides, I wasn't usually involved in those games.

My father said people shied away from me because I was strong and they knew I'd be Alpha one day. He said that meant I needed to make the effort to approach them instead of waiting for them to approach me. Apparently he didn't realize I wasn't waiting for them and I had good reasons.

First off, when I grew up, my job would be to keep an eye on everyone in the pack and make sure they were safe. Starting that habit as a cub would be helpful, I'd decided, and it wasn't something I could do if I was distracted by being part of the fray. Sometimes my father noticed what I was doing and insisted I take a break and have fun. But even then, I had no interest in playing silly games with hyper wolves. Fun meant running free, feeling the wind in my fur, and hunting.

And yet there I was, being dragged through a stranger's house by a boy I didn't know. To make matters worse, he was holding my hand, something only my mother did, and even then, I didn't like it. But though I knew I should pull away, I didn't. Later, when I thought back to that moment, I decided the reason I let him put his hands on me without socking him in the belly was because it was so unexpected.

"Should we race?" Korban asked excitedly as soon as we stepped outside.

I didn't respond.

"Or we can wrestle." He let go of my hand, clasped the back of his T-shirt, and peeled it off. "Or hunt. Are you hungry?" He tossed the shirt aside and kicked off his shoes. "Maybe there's a stream nearby and we can swim." He wiggled out of his pants and briefs in one move and left them where they fell.

With my brain working overtime to absorb all his questions and think about what he probably meant or could mean by each one of them, I hadn't thought to take off my own clothes. So when Korban was finally undressed and ready to shift, I was left looking stupid. Immediately, I realized that had been his goal in distracting me with his litany of questions.

"Why are you still dressed?" His light blond hair was disheveled from when he'd pulled his shirt off. "Did you change your mind about shifting?" He bit his bottom lip. "We don't have to race or, uh, hunt, or whatever. We can do something else."

Because the fact that he caught me off guard so he could get undressed faster meant he could beat me in a footrace in wolf form? No.

"Racing is fine," I bit out. "Hunting too." I looked him straight in the eyes; my father taught me to do that. "We can do both."

Unlike him, I was grateful for my belongings. I carefully unbuttoned my shirt and then folded it before setting it on a small patio table. Then I unlaced my shoes and placed them down under the table with my socks tucked inside. Finally, I removed my briefs and pants and, after folding them neatly, put them next to my shirt. Korban might have undressed faster, but I did it better.

"We'll race to the trees," I told him, making clear right off the bat that being older didn't mean he was in charge. "Then we can track something to eat."

"Okay."

He wasn't smiling, so I figured I'd made my point, which was a good thing. Still, something didn't sit right about it. Thankfully, it didn't last long.

Korban shook his head quickly, like he was in wolf form and was flicking off moisture. Then he grinned again, squeezed my shoulder, and said, "Let's go!"

Surprisingly, he didn't shift midsentence or even after he finished speaking. Instead, he watched me, and only once I'd started taking on my wolf form did he change into his wolf. With his blond hair, it was no surprise I was standing next to a pure white wolf. His eyes were the same navy blue, and even as an animal, they seemed to be twinkling with mirth and laughing at me.

I huffed in frustration, knocked my muzzle against his, and jumped off the porch. I was going to win the race and then I'd track an animal faster and take it down. With that decision made, I ran off toward the trees.

I saw him again when I was twelve and he was fifteen. We were at the next gathering of all the Alphas from our region. I was there with my dad and Korban was there with his.

He looked mostly the same. His hair was still a light blond, but there were more golden streaks in it than when he was younger. His skin was just as pale and seemed to glow, like it had when he was eleven, but I noticed a smattering of freckles over his nose. His eyes, though, were exactly the same. Still a warm navy blue and still tracking me from the second I walked into the room.

"Samuel, hi!" he said as he hustled over to me.

Forcing down the smile that inexplicably started forming, I crossed my arms over my chest. Uncharacteristically, I wanted to say something, but typical to form, I didn't know what would be appropriate. So I remained silent.

"I'm Korban Keller."

He paused.

I didn't say anything. Not because I was trying to be rude, but because my words stuck in my throat. I hated that he was able to force me off-balance so quickly.

"We met at the last Southeast Alphas meeting."

Two seconds in and already he was annoying me. So much so that my belly felt warm. I really did need to get my temper under control.

"We hunted in our wolf forms," he added.

"I remember you," I said coolly and then gave myself an internal pat on the back because I didn't yell at him for assuming I was too dumb to remember someone from four years earlier. It hadn't been that long. Besides, I'd been with him for hours. We had run through the woods, hunted together, splashed in the spring, and even tussled on the grass. It wasn't until later that I realized he had tricked me into letting my guard down.

"Great." He sighed in relief and his shoulders lowered, like he was releasing tension.

Immediately, I wondered why he had been stressed. I darted my gaze around but couldn't see any obvious threats.

"I was hoping your father would bring you again this year, but when you weren't there for the region leader's welcome address, I was worried you weren't going to come."

My father was normally exceptionally punctual. He said being late was a sign of disrespect because it showed you didn't value the other person's time. I always made it a point to get to places early so I wouldn't send that message. But there was no way for my father to have predicted the multicar collision that forced us to wait for the human police and deal with their paperwork.

Not appreciating Korban's need to point out our embarrassing and out-of-character lack of timeliness, I hissed, "We were in an accident. We got here as fast as we could, and it's not like we missed much."

"You were in an accident?" If it was possible for his already alabaster skin to lose color, it did. "Are you okay?" He leaned forward and gently touched my shoulder.

My mind shot back to that day four years prior, when he had grabbed my hand. Clearly, the guy had an issue with personal boundaries. Then again, maybe it was my issue. Other shifters seemed to touch each other freely. With my thoughts occupied, I forgot to answer him.

"You weren't hurt, were you?" he asked.

The question refocused my attention on him, and I noticed he was reaching his hand toward my cheek. My first instinct was to lean toward his touch, but as soon as I realized what I was doing, I jerked back.

"I'm fine!" I snapped. "My father is a great driver. It wasn't his fault."

"Okay. Good." He dragged his hand through his shaggy hair. "You had me worried there for a second."

I narrowed my eyes. "Why?"

"Because you're—" He slammed his mouth shut, blinked rapidly, and then cleared his throat. "Because you're the only other kid who comes to these things. The other Alphas don't bring their next-in-line until they're adults, and sometimes not until they're almost ready to take over the position."

That was true. My father brought me along because he knew I'd be well-behaved and it was important to me—to both of us—that I learn everything I could to lead the pack well. I didn't know why Korban's father brought him. Whatever the reason, it bugged me that he only wanted to spend time with me because there was no alternative. I mean, I didn't want to hang out with him anyway, but still, it was rude to come right out and shove that in my face.

At home, the other kids had more grace than to be so overt about not wanting to be close friends with me. With them, I never felt like they didn't like me, more that we didn't have much in common and I intimidated them. That was what my parents always said.

But there was no way I intimidated Korban Keller. He was older and he had those navy eyes. Plus, I knew his type. He had one of those shiny personalities everybody liked. And with him being groomed to be Alpha of his pack, we did have something in common. So his considering me a last option stung more than usual.

"Well, maybe you'll get lucky and another Alpha will show up late with a son and you can hang out with him." I stepped around him and started stomping away.

"Wait." Korban grasped my shoulder.

I twisted my head around, glanced at his hand and then at his face, and arched one eyebrow.

"I didn't mean it like that," he said.

Though I was taken aback by how easily he had figured out my annoyance and the reason for it, I knew it was exactly how he had meant it.

"I'm sorry if I hurt your feelings."

What he was sorry about was that he had dropped his "perfect guy" act. Still, I couldn't let him think he had impacted me. I needed to be strong, not sensitive.

"Please," I scoffed. "I'd have to care about what you think for that to matter."

He winced and then closed his eyes and took a deep breath before opening them and meeting my gaze. "Well, I guess that's good." He grinned. "What should we do?"

After turning the question over every which way, I still didn't understand what he was asking. He did it on purpose, I was certain—phrased things in weird ways to make me feel stupid. Well, I wasn't going to give him the satisfaction of knowing I cared or even noticed.

"Do?" I said, hoping I sounded nonchalant rather than frustrated.

"Yeah, during the meeting. Do you want to shift and hunt again?" He stepped closer to me, forcing me to raise my chin so I could keep looking him in the eyes. "That was really fun last time," he said quietly. "I've thought about that day a lot."

My stomach heated again, only this time it felt like a burn. I told myself it was from the seat belt tightening around me during the accident, but I knew that didn't make sense. I had felt fine until Korban started talking to me. Because he hadn't given me anything to eat or drink, I knew he hadn't poisoned me, but it was possible I was allergic to something in his scent.

My body wanted to test that theory, it seemed, because without conscious thought, I inhaled deeply. The warmth in my stomach spread lower, and my muscles spasmed. I snapped my gaze up, confused and a little scared.

"Samuel?" Korban said worriedly as he stepped closer to me. "Are you okay?" He put his hand on my cheek and that, combined with his scent, undid me.

It was the best and worst feeling of my life: relief, elation, and satisfaction, followed almost immediately by terror, disgust, and guilt. Reflexively, I squeezed my eyes shut, and all of a sudden, I felt a strange sensation in my pants. My first thought was that I wet myself. It was the only thing that made sense, the only thing my penis had been used for up to that point.

"I'm, uh"—I blinked rapidly and looked everywhere but at Korban—"fine but I need to use the bathroom." I gulped and slowly moved my hands in front of my groin, hoping the change in stance wasn't noticeable. "Do you know where it is?"

"Sure," he said. "I'll show you." He wrapped his arm loosely around my shoulders and led me down the hallway.

Had I been thinking clearly, I would have shoved him away or told him off, but my heart was racing, my briefs were wet, and my groin still felt funny. In a haze, I went along quietly, letting him take me to a bathroom at the far end of the house. He turned the handle, held the door open, and gently nudged me inside.

"Samuel," he said quietly.

I looked back at him over my shoulder.

"It's going to be fine."

I had no idea what he meant, but then I never seemed to know what he meant.

"Maybe not right now, but eventually, it'll be fine." My confusion obviously showed on my face, because he smiled once again, this one gentle and understanding. "I promise. I'll take care of things. No matter what, you'll be fine." He started closing the door slowly. "I'll wait outside and give you some privacy."

Later, I realized the wetness wasn't urine and the feeling wasn't due to an allergy. Though I doubted Korban knew what had happened, my feelings of discomfort around him were exacerbated by that incident. I felt like he'd seen me during a personal and vulnerable time, like he'd intentionally tried to confuse and disarm me and I lacked the control to stop him, and like something was very wrong about him or the way I reacted to him or both. Whatever the case, I made an effort to stay away and I hated him for forcing me to tuck my tail between my legs and hide.

The hate—I found over the years—was much easier to handle, much more comfortable and safe than the storm of confusion it replaced.

CHAPTER 2

YEARS CAME and went but very little changed in my life. My focus remained on developing the skills I'd need to lead the Yafenack pack. My father worked on it with me, which was very helpful, even if he kept nagging at me to socialize. I knew he felt guilty that Eddie and Jen, my younger brother and sister, had more free time and fewer responsibilities and I spent my days and evenings on work instead of play, but I told him I was happy with things as they were. Unfortunately, that assurance never satisfied him.

Which was why, shortly after I finished high school, he sent me into the proverbial lion's den. In reality, it was a wolf's party. Though for all the anxiety and aggravation it caused me, a room full of lions would have been preferable.

"Taking one evening off isn't going to make any difference, Samuel," my mother said as she handed me a napkin. "Wipe your mouth."

"I'm a man now," I pointed out, not that she'd forgotten about my eighteenth birthday the month prior. After all, she'd birthed me. "It's important I work even harder." I took a big bite of the steak sandwich she'd made for me.

"You work hard all the time."

"That's because I'm going to be Alpha of our pack," I pointed out while I chewed.

"Yes. In about ten years or so," she said, her tone a mix of sarcasm and amusement.

It was true. Usually people didn't take over as Alpha until they were in their late twenties or early thirties. So with me being eighteen, my father was years away from stepping down and handing the pack over to me. That was good because I wasn't ready, which was all the more reason I couldn't waste valuable training time.

My mother, of course, would have no idea what that felt like—knowing you were intended to lead, having prepared for it your entire life, but feeling in your core that something was missing. That sense of being lacking had gotten progressively stronger over the years, when it should have been the other way around. No presumptive Alpha worked harder than me; my father even said so. And yet I knew, and he knew, and sometimes I thought the pack knew, that I wasn't ready to lead them.

Feeling frustrated, I sighed and said, "You wouldn't understand."

"I wouldn't understand?" she asked, crossing her arms over her chest and arching her eyebrows. "I've been mated to your father since I was about your age. I think I understand better than just about anybody what it means to be an Alpha."

"Mother," I sighed. "I realize you mean well, but not being an Alpha means you don't truly know our responsibilities."

She couldn't know how difficult it was to balance strength, power, and decisiveness with what my father called empathy, compassion, and flexibility. To me, the traits seemed conflicting, and no matter how much I tried to act empathetic or compassionate, no matter how well I restrained my anger when people didn't do what they were supposed to and things didn't go according to plan, my father was always able to see through me. There were times when

I wondered if I'd ever be able to master the roles he said an Alpha needed to fill well enough to please him.

Shaking my head at my mother, I said, "You don't get it."

"What is it you don't get this time, Johanna?" my father asked as he walked into the kitchen.

"What it means to be an Alpha," she said, tilting her head to the side to make room for the kiss he would give her.

He always kissed her after they'd been apart. Even if it was only for a couple of hours. I didn't understand it, but it wasn't relevant to me, so I didn't give it much thought.

"Is that right?" My parents shared a knowing look and smiled. It was one of their inside jokes.

I took another bite of my sandwich.

"Yes." She nodded. "It's amazing, isn't it, Tom, how much less we know as the kids get older?"

My father laughed and nodded. Then he turned to me and said, "Do you need me to drive you to the gathering, or do you want to take the car?"

"Oh, uh, you know what? I don't need to waste your time driving me or borrow the car and leave you stranded so, uh, why don't I stay home? I don't mind. We can work on, uh..." I tried to think of what he'd most like me to work on. "How to force... No." I shook my head. He didn't like when I phrased things that way. "How to inspire pack members to listen to me." I tensed, waiting for his reply.

"Nice try, kiddo," he said, ruffling my hair.

I growled under my breath. "I'm not a kid."

"Well, all right. It's decided." My father grinned, his green eyes sparkling.

My eyes were green too, and I liked to tell myself they were like his, but they were actually lighter, flatter somehow. Our hair was the same shade of chocolate brown, though.

"Do you want to get a jacket?" my mother asked. "It might get chilly out at night."

"Chilly? What do you mean?" I darted my gaze back and forth between the two of them, certain I'd successfully steered them against my going to the gathering and therefore feeling like I'd missed something. "Where are we going?"

"You said you're an adult," my father said. "That means you won't hide away in here."

Completing his thought, as usual, my mother said, "You'll go meet with the other young adults from our pack and the neighboring packs. And you'll have fun."

"But—"

My mother turned her attention away from me and focused on my father. "You're home earlier than I expected, Tom." She smoothed out his shirt with her palms. "I thought you had a late meeting with that human about the road."

Our pack lands were relatively small, but they were ours. We'd lived on the land for generations without owning it. That changed when my grandfather was Alpha. He had insisted that land ownership was the way of the future and would ensure the security of the pack. From what my father taught me, it had been difficult and somewhat controversial at the time, but my grandfather hadn't backed down. And history had proven him right, because for as long as I could remember, Yafenack had been a small but strong pack.

My father's new attempt at growth wasn't about land, but instead about money. He had learned from a friend and fellow Alpha that interacting with humans would help our pack prosper. I'd never met

Zev Hassick, the Alpha of the Etzgadol pack, but I'd heard of him. He had taken an already good-sized, well-respected, strong pack and improved it. From what I understood, their numbers were growing, their members were prospering, and their Alpha was responsible for both.

Wanting to better our pack, my father had been meeting with the humans about a private road that would connect our pack lands to their highway. The pack would build it and maintain it, and the humans would make sure it wasn't a marked exit. He also planned to put up fencing a short ways in to block strangers from coming in but still allow us easy access to the outside world. Secluded but connected, that was my father's philosophy.

"We met about the road and agreed to go through with it," my father said. "I told the human we could finalize the details next week." He looked at me. "I wanted to make sure I got home in time to drive you to the young adult gathering."

"How long?" I asked resignedly.

My father glanced at the clock on the wall. "We should leave pretty soon. It starts at seven, and the roads from here to Miancarem wind so much the drive will be close to an hour."

I had meant how long I had to stay, but given his answer, I decided against clarifying.

"Hey!" I straightened up in my chair. "I have an idea."

"What's that?" my father asked.

"I can shift and run over to the gathering. If I take the woods instead of the roads, I can cut the time in half."

"Uh-huh," my mother said, her tone disbelieving. "And what will you do when you get there?"

"What do you mean?"

My father elaborated for her. "You'll arrive at the gathering in wolf form, which means you'll have no clothes."

"Oh, that's okay." I waved them off. "I don't mind staying in wolf form."

"Of course he doesn't," my mother said. She shook her head and walked over to the fridge.

"Of course you don't," my father said at the same time. Then he sighed. "Samuel, part of being a strong shifter is being a strong man."

"I'm strong!" I hopped out of my chair. "I was the strongest wolf in my school, Dad. You know that!"

"Yes, I do." He nodded. "But I said a strong man."

At five foot eleven inches and one hundred fifty-five pounds, I wasn't huge, but I was fit. I made sure to exercise and stay in shape.

"I don't mean your body, Samuel," my father said, apparently knowing where my thoughts had gone. "I'm talking about in here." He tapped his chest. "You prefer being in your wolf form."

I opened my mouth to deny it, but he kept talking.

"I know it's true. I've noticed you're always the last to shift back after runs these days."

He was right about the shifting, but it wasn't because I wanted to stay in my wolf form. It was because my wolf form didn't want to relinquish its hold on my body. I would have explained that to my father, but I didn't know how to say it in a way that made sense.

"And I understand why you're doing it."

I looked at him and widened my eyes in surprise. He knew about how my wolf clung to my form? How I felt itchy if I went too long without shifting? Did that mean it was normal? Maybe it was an Alpha characteristic. Of course, then I'd have seen it in the writings I diligently studied…

"An Alpha's job is to support the members so everyone can work together toward bettering the pack. To support them and elevate them, you have to know them. You're uncomfortable talking with people, Samuel. Our pack included."

Well, there was that too. I dipped my chin and focused on moving the crumbs around on my plate.

"That has always been your biggest challenge, and we've spent many years working on it," my father said gently. "But you're eighteen now, and it's getting harder to explain to the pack."

"They know?" I jerked my head up. "Who told them?"

"Nobody told them, but, son, they're starting to notice." My father dragged his fingers through his hair. "When you were a cub, it was different. They thought I was overprotective or you were shy. But now you're a man and their presumptive Alpha, and they have no connection to you."

"No connection? I've lived among them since I was born. I've dedicated my life to becoming the best Alpha they can have. How can they—"

"I know, Samuel." My father reached across the table and took hold of my hand. "And if it came to a physical challenge, you'd win. You'd also best anyone, myself included, in a battle about pack history or shifter culture."

"No, I wouldn't. You're the best—"

"You know more about our past and our rules. It won't be long before you're stronger than me. But there is more to leading than being the best physically and most knowledgeable intellectually."

I knew that already, because he had been telling me the same thing for years. I didn't fully agree with him, but I'd never say that out loud.

"Part of being a good Alpha is strength, but another is compassion and tenderness. We need to lead with a velvet hammer, not an iron fist." He tapped his chest again. "You have to connect, Samuel. You have to feel for your pack."

"I do," I insisted. "I know everyone's name, the ages of their children, where they work—"

"Yes. That you do." My father nodded and patted my hand. "I've seen your notecards, son. I know how hard you work on memorizing those things and on everything else." He looked sad, but I didn't know why.

My mother sighed behind me.

"I'm going to drive Samuel to Miancarem, and then I'll be back." My father stood and walked over to her. He kissed her cheek, as if they wouldn't see each other for days, and then looked at me. "Let's go."

I should have known he'd be there. He was, after all, the son of the Miancarem Alpha. But for some reason, I had expected only shifters my age and maybe a year older to be at the young adult gathering, not those who were out of their teens.

Korban Keller had turned twenty-one on January 3. Somewhere along the way, I'd heard his birthday and, despite my best efforts, I'd never forgotten it. And I'd tried.

Most of the shifters congregated next to two big bonfires in the clearing. With everyone standing close together, it took me a few moments to see Korban in the center of the crowd. By the time I noticed him, it was too late to turn back without seeming like a coward in front of him and my peers, so I didn't dash back to the car, even though that was exactly what I wanted to do.

Instead, I settled for quickly darting my gaze over my shoulder to my father, who was about to drive off, and saying in a loud whisper, "One hour, okay? Come get me in an hour."

"Samuel, that's not long enough. The others will be here until the moon is high in the sky, maybe later."

"Please," I said desperately, certain Korban had spotted me and was staring at me with those navy eyes. I was turned away from him, so I couldn't confirm that visually, but I felt his gaze over every inch of my skin.

"I'll be back at ten," my father said. "And I hope when I do, you'll tell me you want to stay later." His forehead creased with worry. "Please, Samuel. Try."

He drove off, and I was alone with Korban Keller. Well, I was alone with Korban Keller and dozens of other shifters. But he was the only one I noticed. And I still wasn't looking in his direction.

Was it shame that made me hyperaware of Korban, or was it my intuition warning me that he was dangerous? I had behaved oddly the other times we'd met, and even though six years had passed since I'd last seen him—I had intentionally avoided going to the regional Alphas' meeting two years prior—the memories of the time I spent with him were vivid in my mind.

Remembering those hours made me intensely uncomfortable, and yet I'd never been able to stop myself from thinking about them. In the end, I didn't know why I reacted to Korban the way I did, only that it was wrong, that he was wrong, and that I needed to stay away from him. And yet, despite all the reasons I'd come up with to avoid the gathering, the possibility that I might see Korban hadn't crossed my mind.

By twenty-one, most shifters were paired off, if not already married. Although the young adult gathering wasn't stated to be a place exclusively for singles, it was understood that, after high school, we were at the age to find a mate, and because packs were generally small, it was helpful to meet other shifters in the area and, hopefully, find a suitable match. Maybe Korban was there because he was still single—another thing I inexplicably knew about him and unfortunately couldn't forget.

Reaching deep within myself, I called on my training and schooled my features. I was going to be Alpha. That meant I had to appear controlled, strong, and confident. The members of my pack had to have faith in my ability to lead, and the members of the other packs had to know I wasn't someone to be challenged. With those reminders front and center in my mind, I turned around and looked at the shifters gathered around the fires, and not at Korban.

Based on my quick assessment, everyone was huddled with their own packs. It made sense that early in the night, people would still be with those they knew. I also confirmed my suspicion about the ages of the shifters present, at least with regard to the members of the Yafenack pack. Only shifters who had graduated with me and those who had graduated the year prior were there, and all of them were single.

So unless the other packs were including a larger age group in the gathering, there was no reason for Korban to be there. I owed it to my pack to monitor him and make sure he wouldn't do anything unscrupulous. Trying to remain inconspicuous, I glanced at him from the corner of my eye. He was laughing and holding court, surrounded by what looked like adoring fans who hung on his every word and, though it was too dark and he was too far away for me to be certain, he seemed to be staring at me. Damn him for putting me on edge once again.

I was so distracted by Korban's presence that I somehow missed the other person outside of my age group at the gathering.

"Samuel Goodwin, isn't it?"

I flipped around at the sound of the voice right behind me and saw Dirk Keller, Korban's father and Alpha of the Miancarem pack.

"Oh, uh, Mr. Keller, hello." My voice went a little high-pitched at the end, so I cleared my throat, sucked in a deep breath, and reminded myself never to show weakness to a potential adversary. "Thank you for hosting this gathering," I said, internally patting myself on the back for remembering my manners. "The Yafenack pack is grateful." I could speak on behalf of the pack. My father was Alpha, after all, and he was always telling me how important it was to remember the pack would eventually be mine to lead.

"Was that your father I saw rushing off?" he said.

I didn't like his tone. "Yes." I nodded. "He drove me here."

"I'm surprised he didn't take the time to say hello to me." He didn't look at my face as he spoke, instead looking over my shoulder to where my father's car had been. "But I gather he's too busy rubbing elbows with half-souls to have time to greet a fellow Alpha."

"He didn't realize you were here," I said quickly, wanting to make sure my father didn't come across as rude. He abhorred rudeness in any form.

He also detested the use of the term half-soul, saying it was derogatory to humans. We'd learned never to say the epithet in our house, but occasionally, I still heard it from pack members. If they uttered it within hearing distance of my father, they were swiftly reprimanded. I didn't feel it would be appropriate for me to do the same to the Miancarem Alpha on his own pack lands, so I focused on explaining my father's behavior.

"We understood the gathering to be for young adults only," I said, glancing toward the spot where Korban had been standing. He was gone. A chill washed over me. "But I'll, uh, make sure to pass on your regards."

"What regard?" he scoffed. "I heard from Phillip Jones that Tom Goodwin is continuing to meet with half-souls. I have no regard for that."

Phillip Jones was the brother of Patrick Jones, one of our new pack members. He'd joined us about a year earlier, he and his family. Reflecting back, I remembered my father saying he'd come over from the Miancarem pack. I hadn't asked why because it wasn't that unusual; we'd had several different families move over from their pack to ours. I assumed it was the nature of being relatively near each other. Although when I thought about it, I realized I couldn't recall anyone leaving the Yafenack pack other than a couple of people who had mated with someone from a distant pack.

Before I could figure out how to respond to Dirk Keller, I felt heat at my back.

"Father." It was Korban. His voice was deeper than the last time I'd heard it, but it was still familiar. And his scent... I'd know it anywhere. "I didn't realize you'd be here."

"It's my pack, Korban." He bristled. "You're not yet of age to take over."

In my entire life, my father had never reacted to me that way. It was as if Dirk Keller didn't want his son to step into his shoes. I furrowed my brow in confusion and shuffled to the side, looking back and forth between Korban and his father.

"That's true." Korban moved forward, shouldering his way past me and standing directly between me and his father.

Because he was a couple of inches taller than me, he effectively cut off my view, which was rude. No surprise. I stepped back, needing to put distance between us and curious enough about the dynamic between him and his father that I wanted to watch them both.

"But I'm closer in age to the shifters here, so it was decided the visitors would be more comfortable with my presence," Korban said.

"It was decided?" Dirk spat.

Korban nodded. "I believe I mentioned it to you."

"You did," Dirk admitted. "And so did several others." His jaw ticced. "But it's my pack, so I felt it was important to make an appearance."

"Yes, sir." Korban's words were respectful but his tone was not. That was no way to speak to your Alpha or your father. The man had neither manners nor honor. "Thank you for stopping by. I'll give you a full report tomorrow."

With a grunt, Dirk stalked off. Korban turned and glared at his retreating form. And, without my conscious realization, I stared at Korban.

"Samuel," he said, finally turning his gaze to me once his father was gone. "I'm so pleased to see you again. It's been too long." He reached forward slowly and squeezed my shoulder. "I heard you've been doing well. Graduated at the top of your class." He grinned. "Very impressive."

How did he know that? Who was reporting information about me? And why did he need the information? Before I could ask those questions, he dragged his gaze up and down my body, distracting me.

"You look great." His voice was husky, and when he returned his focus to my face, I noticed his pupils were dilated. What was going on? Was he going to shift? "Listen." He licked his lips and swallowed hard. "I know you're here for the gathering and—"

"Yes." The reminder snapped me back into the present. "It's important for me to support the Yafenack pack and to meet the members of the other packs in our region. I'm going to be Alpha." I paused, realizing in light of the conversation he'd just had with his own father that I may have sounded silly given my younger age. It'd be a decade yet before I'd take over for my father. "Eventually."

"I know." Korban still had his hand on my shoulder, and he squeezed it again. "And you'll make a terrific Alpha." His expression was sincere, which made no sense. "Do you think maybe you have a few minutes to spend with me before you join your pack?"

"Why?" Why did he want to spend time with me? And why did I want to say yes? "Is it so we can network?"

"Network?" He sounded confused by the concept, but then he smiled one of his huge smiles, the one that lit up his face and forced me to remind myself that he was fake and I hated him. "Sure. We can network."

It would have been rude and insulting to say no, so I agreed.

CHAPTER 3

"I STILL DON'T understand how he can blame you for it," I said to my father. "They come to our pack on their own volition. If he doesn't like losing members, Dirk Keller should ask them why they leave Miancarem instead of getting angry at the Alphas of the packs they join."

"Dirk doesn't ask because he already knows the answer, or at least he thinks he does. And he blames me because it's easier to claim the problem is someone leading his members astray or having better land or resources than to take responsibility for the way he's managing his pack." My father snorted. "Hell, it's easier than taking responsibility for the way the last few Alphas have led that pack. Some of the stories I heard from my father..." He shook his head.

"Miancarem's pack lands are great," I argued. "They're not as secluded as ours, but they have a large area and a nice gap before the human town starts."

I'd noticed that two years prior when I'd attended the young adults gathering and ended up shifting into my wolf form with Korban Keller. We'd only been talking for a few minutes when I suddenly started feeling heated. I'd been short of breath too. And my skin seemed too tight.

Thankfully, Korban had suggested shifting and going for a run. I had readily agreed, needing to do something, anything, to prevent the future Alpha from seeing me in a less than healthy condition.

We'd run through the woods in the Miancarem pack lands and all the way up to the human town.

Even though I wasn't alone, which was my preference during runs—and any other time—I'd enjoyed myself. In fact, I couldn't remember the last time I'd felt so exhilarated during a run. Well, maybe I could, but that had been different. That was back when I was an eight-year-old kid proving myself to... I shook my head and focused on my father.

"Yes, the Miancarem pack lands are great. But that's not good enough for Dirk." My father looked at me meaningfully. "Some people are like that, Samuel. Nothing is enough for them; everyone has something better in their mind and they resent not having it too." He sighed. "Doesn't matter. We need to focus on you right now, not on the Miancarem pack. I want you to shift so I can see what's happening. But first, explain to me one more time what's going on inside you when you shift back to human."

Though I hadn't told him, my father had noticed I was having trouble with my shift from wolf to human. It had been building slowly, so slowly I hadn't noticed it at first. Eventually it became too obvious to miss. So much so that I'd started making sure to shift back on my own, hiding behind the house or trees so nobody would witness how long it took me to relinquish my wolf form and force myself back into my human skin. My father was observant, though, so he caught on.

I wasn't surprised, but I wished I could have kept it hidden a bit longer, sure that with a little more time and a little more research, I could have resolved whatever caused my problem and he wouldn't have had to know about it. Changing the topic seemed to be my only chance at a distraction.

"What do you mean leading his members astray? What does Dirk Keller think you're doing?"

Turning toward the trees, my father crossed his arms over his chest and looked out into the woods. "It's impossible to know what he actually thinks, but from what I've heard, it's mostly based on our interaction with humans. He believes that by working with them and acknowledging their power over certain things—like their roads—we're disregarding our culture and heritage, tossing away our traditions, and degrading ourselves."

I tilted my head and furrowed my brow. "There's nothing in the writings about our traditions and culture that says we can't work with humans." I was sure of it. I'd pored over every writing I could find as part of my Alpha studies and read them so much I had them memorized practically word for word. When my time came to be Alpha, I'd be prepared both in body and in mind. I'd know about our past so I could lead us to a stronger future.

"You were the only teenager I'd ever seen who preferred combing through old texts to watching television." My father laughed. "I'm sure you could school me and every other pack Alpha about shifter history."

He reached forward to ruffle my hair, but I stepped back. I was twenty, a man. Sometimes he forgot, so I had to remind him.

"The thing about culture, though," he continued, "is it isn't always written down."

"What do you mean? If it matters, it's in the texts."

"Not necessarily. Some things you only learn by talking to people."

Of course, he would once again bring the conversation around to interacting more with the pack. With everything I did right, I kept hoping he'd be satisfied, but I was forever coming up short on that part of my training.

I hated letting my father down, but no matter how hard I tried to play the part of Alpha as he described it to me, even going as far as using his words verbatim when I spoke with pack members, he said I wasn't leading from the heart and the pack would sense it. When I asked him how to act like I was leading from the heart, he shook his head, said it wasn't about acting, and looked disappointed. So I stopped asking questions, deciding I'd figure it out on my own. Up to that point, I hadn't made any progress, but, thankfully, I still had years before I'd start my time as Alpha.

"The parts of culture you witness are just as important as the ones you read in the writings." My father paused and knitted his eyebrows in thought. "There are things you learn by hearing people talk when they don't realize you're listening, by seeing how they act when they're not thinking about it. You learn how your pack sees things based on what they say and do when they feel free to be themselves."

I had no idea what he meant. I was always aware of what I said and who was around. After all, the only reason I was with people or spoke to them was because it was part of my training and would be part of my responsibility as Alpha. There was nothing freeing about that. Only when I was alone in my room could I relax; but then I didn't speak out loud. Nobody could read my thoughts, so that couldn't be what my father meant.

"Do you hide so they don't know you can hear them?" I asked, thinking that was his point. "Is that how you always know what the pack members need? Is it part of monitoring them and—"

"Of course not," my father snapped, catching me off guard. "That's not what I..." He looked at me, and his expression changed from anger to one I'd seen many times but never fully understood. It resembled concern or sadness. "During unguarded moments, simple conversations, people say what they take for granted as being normal," he explained in a lower, calmer tone. I thought of it as his teaching voice. "And then you realize some shifters have taken the tradition of pride and connection with the pack and transformed it into animosity toward those who aren't pack. But they're wrong. The pack is stronger when we're connected with the world around us, and we can't connect if we refuse to acknowledge others, or if we degrade them by calling them names or—"

"That's why you tell the pack not to call humans half-souls," I mumbled, talking more to myself than to him.

"Exactly. Lowering those around us does not elevate us. Our pride, our strength—" He looked me in the eyes and tapped his chest. "It needs to come from within or it's flimsy and meaningless."

Nodding in understanding, I committed the lesson to memory so I could reflect on it later. I'd probably write it down in the Alpha studies journal I kept so I could go back to it when it was my turn to lead.

"All done with the questions now?" my father asked after a few moments of silence. "Or do you have something else to distract me from working with you on the shifting issue?"

He knew what I'd been up to. Of course he knew. My father knew everything. It was why he was such a good Alpha. I lowered my gaze in shame.

"There's nothing else." I gulped. "I can shift now."

"Okay." He nodded. "Shift into your wolf, go for a quick run, and then shift back. I'll watch you."

Nodding, I pushed down my shorts and briefs and folded them.

"Samuel."

I glanced up at my father as I put my clothes on the table we kept on the back porch.

"I want you to pay close attention to how you're feeling during both shifts—into your wolf form and back to your human. When you're done, explain it to me so we can understand what's going on."

"It's the only thing that makes sense, Tom," my mother said.

"Do you really think so?" He started pacing. Not that I could see him from my perch behind the wall outside the kitchen entry, but it sounded like pacing. "I had the same thought, but he's so young."

"He is twenty years old," my mother reminded him.

I nodded vehemently, even though nobody could see me.

"When we were his age, I was pregnant with him," she added.

"You're right." I heard the chair scrape across the linoleum floor. "It's hard to remember sometimes."

I wasn't sure why it was so hard with me constantly reminding him.

"He's our son, but he's also a man." My chest puffed up with pride in response to my mother's comment. "You need to talk to him before things get worse."

Worse? I was barely able to shift back into my human skin as it was. How could things get worse?

"You're right, Johanna," my father said.

"Good." I heard her patting him—his chest or his leg, probably. That was what she usually did. "Do you want me to stay here?"

"No. This will be difficult enough for him without his mother in the room."

What were they talking about?

"I agree." She kissed him. "I'm going up to bed. Good night."

I heard my mother's footsteps approaching and quickly turned around, ready to dash to my bedroom.

"Samuel," my father called out. "Come on in here."

I froze in place. He couldn't know I was there. There was no way. I'd been quiet, and in my own home, my scent was everywhere, so my presence couldn't be distinguished that way.

"Samuel," he said again.

Before I could decide what to do, my mother stepped out of the kitchen.

"He's waiting." She smiled at me. "Don't worry. Everything will be fine."

I watched her as she walked away, and then I reminded myself I was a strong man and cowering in the dark was unbecoming. Of course, I'd been doing that very thing, and eavesdropping to boot, but it hadn't been intentional. I'd come downstairs to get water and—

"Samuel!"

I hurried into the kitchen.

"Have a seat." My father pointed at the chairs around the small table but didn't take one for himself. Instead, he paced. "There's no easy way to ask this, so I'm going to go ahead and just ask it."

Something about his tone made me realize sitting down would be a good idea, so I did.

"Have you tied yet?"

The question didn't make sense. Or my brain froze.

"Samuel?" He pulled out a chair and sat down across from me. "Have you ever tied with anyone?"

Understanding what he was asking, I lowered my gaze and felt my cheeks heat.

"There's no shame in it, son. Like I've told you before, sex is natural. It's part of who you are."

Yes, he had told me that on more than one occasion. But I'd been younger then, and once puberty was over, I thought we were done with those horrible conversations.

When I didn't answer, he sighed in frustration. "Eddie and Jen are still in their teens, and you see how freely they discuss sex. Son, you're twenty."

I remembered my brother and sister being sat down for the same lesson when they'd each been about twelve, but neither of them had looked as uncomfortable as I had been during the talk. Now at thirteen and fourteen, they were demonstrative with their affections and had no trouble talking about the lessons they'd been taught.

"Samuel?" My father sighed. "I've known this is a difficult subject for you, so I haven't pushed it. That was wrong of me and I'm sorry. I failed you."

I snapped my gaze up, shocked that he thought he'd done something wrong. "No, I—"

"Yes," he said firmly. "It's my fault. I realize you're...different about some things, including touching or talking about touching, but Samuel, you need to listen to me now."

He looked and sounded serious, so I forced myself to meet his gaze.

"When shifters reach adulthood, we need to tie so we can hold on to both parts of ourselves."

I rolled my eyes at his statement of the obvious. I knew everything there was to know about our kind.

"From the expression on your face, I take it you already know this."

"Of course I know! Dad, I study harder than any—"

"Nobody is questioning your dedication or your knowledge, Samuel."

I calmed down.

"Now answer my question."

And I was back to being tense. He was my father and my Alpha, but the question felt invasive. Besides, I was ashamed of my answer.

"Isn't that a little, um"—I fidgeted in my seat—"personal?"

"Fine." My father sighed and dragged his hand through his hair. "Let me put it in a way you'll understand. When you read about shifters and tying, what did you learn about male shifters after they reach adulthood?"

Talking about my studies was much easier than talking about myself. Sitting up straight, I cleared my throat. "Shifters' souls straddle two bodies: the wolf and the human," I recited. "Males are more connected to their wolf halves, which is why males have control over that form from childhood and begin taking their wolf forms as young cubs. But for males to retain their human forms after adulthood, they have to tie with female shifters and connect with part of their humanity. Female shifters are more connected to their human half, so they can't shift as cubs. They take their wolf forms only after accepting ties from males."

My father stared at me, his eyebrows raised. I felt like I was missing a question.

"Samuel, you're having trouble shifting back into your human form," he reminded me.

"Uh-huh."

"Well, the simple reason for that could be that you haven't tied yet."

My stomach plunged. "Oh," I whispered.

"I don't want to make you uncomfortable, but you're twenty years old. Surely you want to have sex. Is it that you're too shy to approach anyone? Because I'm sure your mother could help. Ask her for advice. She can tell you what to say. I know she's tried to make suggestions many times."

I lowered my gaze, unable to look him in the face. There had to be something wrong with me. Something worse than having trouble shifting back into my human form.

"Son?" he said, his voice strained. "Don't you want to tie?"

The truth was, I didn't want to, and even if I did, I was pretty sure I wouldn't be able to do it. There was a female I'd met about a year prior, outside of our pack. I'd been traveling with my family to visit old friends of my parents. She lived nearby. Somehow we kept ending up alone together, and one night she tried to kiss me. Before her lips could connect with mine, I backed away.

But then she talked about tying and said I was handsome. Other shifters my age had been having sex for a few years already, so I'd forced myself to stay still, forced myself to let her touch me. Based on what I'd heard others say, I'd expected to feel pleasure, arousal, an erection. But none of those things happened. Instead, when her hands wandered below my beltline, I felt so sick I was sure I'd throw up. So I ran.

Maybe if I explained that to my father, he'd be able to help me. "Remember that female who lived close to the Harrisons?"

It took him a moment but then he nodded. "Yes." Suddenly his face lit up. "Yes! You two spent a lot of time together when we visited Etzgadol." He sighed in relief and grasped my shoulder.

"Thank heavens. You had me scared for a minute there. I thought you hadn't ever tied and didn't want to."

I hadn't ever tied and didn't want to. But no way was I going to admit that after seeing my father's reaction. I didn't want to lie to him either, though, so instead, I stayed still and quiet, silently praying he'd move on and let it go. I got half my wish.

"Of course if tying isn't the issue, it means something else is going on with you." He furrowed his brow in thought. "From what you told me, the trouble with your shifting started quite some time before we took that trip and it's never gotten better." He looked at me expectantly.

I nodded in confirmation because his statement was true.

"And I assume you've tied again since? Not with her, of course, but once you start, you can't stop, eh?" He chuckled and slapped my back, like we were old buddies.

It was nice. What was even nicer was that he didn't seem to expect an answer.

"Let me chew on this some more, Samuel. We'll figure it out."

"Okay." I got up. "Thank you."

While he worked on figuring out whether there was something else wrong with me, I'd work on figuring out how to fix what I already knew was broken because what he said made sense. The books were clear—a male shifter needed to tie with a female shifter to hold on to his humanity. I was a male shifter. That meant no matter how much I detested having people touch me, I would be strong and find a way to tie.

CHAPTER 4

I NEVER FOUND a way to tie. It wasn't that I didn't know how. Though I'd dismissed my father's attempts to talk to me in any sort of detail about something so personal, I hadn't had any trouble finding information about sex. After all, I had a computer.

Most shifters had, at best, a grudging acceptance of technology, preferring the trees and the land and the air to being indoors in front of a screen. I had always loved being in my wolf form too, much more than my human form. But with my shifting issue intensifying, I could no longer risk following the call of my wolf for fear that I wouldn't be able to return to my human skin.

When I went outside and smelled the fresh air and soil and trees, the need to become one with nature and feel my paws on the ground was overwhelming, so I had taken to staying indoors. Getting an education seemed like a perfect thing to do with my free time, but my Alpha training prevented me from being able to attend a traditional college. Thankfully, I found courses on the Internet and received a degree that way, managing to become very adept at using a computer along the way.

I had always had a head for numbers, and after my first business course, I realized I loved working with spreadsheets. Accounting seemed like a natural career choice, but becoming a good Alpha continued to be my top priority, so I divided my time between my training and school. It had worked out well for me.

Now twenty-three, I had my degree and a job providing accounting services for Internet-based companies. I did all my work via e-mail with a very rare phone call mixed in, and I never had to meet anyone in person. Though I could afford to move out on my own, I was still living with my parents because I hadn't yet mated and I was training under my father.

If I hadn't been dealing with the shifting issue, my life would have been right on track. But with my shifting problem, I never felt right, never felt whole. It was because I was suppressing my wolf, not allowing myself to shift for fear I wouldn't be able to return to my human form.

It was incredibly difficult to smother such an important part of myself, but with a lot of focus, I was able to hold the shift back most of the time. Unfortunately, when I got tired or angry, my control weakened, emotions overrode my common sense, and my wolf broke through. Shifters were generally clear-minded in our wolf form. We were more in touch with nature and our core needs while in our wolf skins, but we still had rational thought, still knew who we were and what we were doing. But my wolf had become unmanageable.

When I shifted, a clawing need, a desperation, a deep sense of frustration overrode all my common sense. Once I was in my wolf form, I'd inexplicably head straight for the woods at a breakneck pace. Normally, going for a run would have been fine, but I inevitably dashed through our pack lands and crossed over into the Miancarem pack lands. With the strained relationship their Alpha, Dirk Keller, had with my father, infiltrating their territory without permission was dangerous and stupid. I'd never considered myself either of those, and yet I continued to lose focus and ended up going exactly where I had no right being.

On more than one occasion, my father and brother had chased me through the forest. They had surrounded me, tackled me, and held me down until I snapped out of the fog in my mind. As I'd gotten older, I'd outgrown my father, so it wasn't easy for them to overpower me, even with two of them and only one of me. Thankfully, they'd managed to do it and, up to that point, I hadn't been hurt. But I could have been.

My parents were both worried, I knew. They worried for me and, of course, for the pack. I put on a brave face, insisted everything was fine, but I knew it wasn't. My duty to lead the Yafenack pack was getting closer and closer, and despite all my knowledge and training and physical strength, I was in no position to be Alpha. An Alpha had to be strong in both forms. He had to garner the respect of the pack and lead them, not hide indoors because he couldn't control himself.

And that was why I found myself looking in the mirror on yet another Friday morning. I straightened my shirt, brushed my hair, and wondered if that night would be the night my body wouldn't betray me. Every other time I'd made the trek to a gathering far from our pack lands, I'd returned home without success.

Seeking a female to tie with inside my own pack wasn't an option. First off, I knew them all and not one inflamed lust within me. But what was worse, if I tried to ignore my distaste for them and force my body to do what it was meant to do and failed yet again, the female would know and the information would spread through the pack like wildfire. I would not only shame my family, I would decimate my chance to become Alpha if my pack realized I had such little control over my own body.

Trying to keep a positive attitude, I climbed into my car and began the long trek to the annual gathering of the packs in the region north of ours. I had made a point to learn when all the regions had their gatherings and then attended. I'd slip in quietly, never tell anyone what pack I was from, and seek out a female. I had learned early on that females found me attractive, so I never had trouble garnering their interest. The problem was that in order to tie, my body had to cooperate, and time and again, I failed on that count.

It was no different that night, so my mood was already sour when I reached the Yafenack pack lands early the following morning. The long drive had given me time to think about my struggles. I was twenty-three years old, an adult by any standard. I had to tie in order to hold on to my human half, but I couldn't. And because there was no other explanation for my shifting issue, I knew the two struggles were interconnected. I finally admitted to myself that I couldn't solve my shortcomings on my own and I had to confess what had been going on to my father.

An odd sort of calm came over me with that decision. Oh, I was still ashamed and disappointed and scared, but I knew my father would be able to help me just as he always had, and there was peace in that, relief. Unfortunately, it was short-lived.

As soon as I walked into the house, I was slapped with a vision of panic. My family and my father's close friends were rushing around the large entryway, talking loudly and looking stressed.

"What's going on?" I asked nobody in particular.

When I didn't get a response, I darted my gaze around, trying to figure out the answer on my own. The entryway was in the center of the house, surrounded by arched openings leading to the living room, the kitchen, the dining space, my father's study, and a pack gathering room. A curved stairway leading to the bedrooms broke up the space.

With thick pine floors, butter-colored walls, and diamond-shaped windows, the Alpha den was normally warm and calm, much like the Alpha himself. My father was a hard man to ruffle and he was good at soothing the nerves of those around him. Pack members came to him when they were worried or needed advice, and he always found a way to resolve their concerns. Instinctively, I looked for him among the tightly strung people, but I didn't have success.

"Where's Dad?" I said, hoping my mother or brother or sister would finally notice my presence and answer me. One out of three wasn't bad.

"Samuel!" My mother rushed over to me. "I'm so glad you're home. I worried you wouldn't get here in time."

"In time for what?" I fished my phone out of my pocket and looked at my calendar; we had nothing scheduled. "And why didn't you call to tell me"—I had no idea what was happening, so I had no idea what she would have said had she called—"something was going on?"

She flicked her gaze from my face to the phone in my hand and back again. "Oh. I always forget you carry that thing around." She shook her head. "Never mind. It's not important now. Go speak with your father. He's in the study."

Already frustrated with my inability to tie, the long drive, and the disarray in my den, I repeatedly squeezed my hands into fists and released them as I marched toward the study.

"Dad?" I knocked and slowly opened the door.

"Come on in, Samuel."

The overhead lamp was off, so the only illumination in the room came from a stained-glass lamp perched on the corner of the desk my great-grandfather had made by hand from fallen trees from our pack lands. My father was on the other side of the room, sitting on the small brown tweed sofa wedged into the corner.

"Is everything okay?" I stepped toward him. "Everyone seems"—I furrowed my brow, pinched my lips together, and tried to think of a good description—"anxious and worried."

"You can sense their emotions?" he asked, sitting up straight and peering at me, hope flashing in his eyes.

"No." I frowned. "I know Alphas connect with the emotions of their pack," I said, reciting from the writings by memory. "But I thought that happened only after they took their role."

"That's true." My father's forehead crinkled and he nodded slowly. "But the ability sometimes manifests in small measures earlier, and I hoped..." He cleared his throat and shook off the rest of what he was going to say.

Normally, I would have pressed for an explanation and then run upstairs to comb the writings about Alpha powers to see if the ability my father described was documented and I had missed it. As it was, I remained fixated on the flurry of activity on the other side of the door.

"What's going on?" I asked. "Why are all those people here? Why does Mom look scared? Why are you alone in your study? Why—"

"I've been challenged."

I snapped my jaw closed. What did that mean? I tipped my head to the side and stared at my father, flipping through my mental catalogue of possible definitions for that word. There was only one thing I could think of, but it wasn't done, at least not in modern times, so it couldn't be what he meant.

"I don't understand," I finally admitted.

"Yes, you do." My father sighed. "In fact, I'd venture to say you understand better than any living shifter. Nobody knows more about our history, our traditions, and our rules than you. I've been going through the writings, trying to prepare"—he nudged his chin toward the notebooks strewn around him on the couch—"but I'm worried I may have missed something."

"Somebody challenged your standing as Alpha of the Yafenack pack?" I couldn't conceive of that happening. My father was beloved by the entire pack. He was strong and yet compassionate. Smart and yet approachable. Wise but still connected to modern times. And our line... A Goodwin had served as Alpha of our pack all the way back to its inception. "Why?" I asked in disbelief. "Who?"

"Dirk Keller." The "why" didn't need to be answered once he identified the "who." "I can beat him in a fight as both man and wolf," my father assured me. "That isn't my concern." He rubbed his palms over his eyes. "But I need to make sure I understand all the rules." Blinking his eyes open, he drew in a deep breath. "I can't risk disqualification or otherwise being deemed the loser of the battle because of an archaic loophole."

"When's the fight?" I rasped, fear robbing me of my voice.

"This evening."

"That soon? But there has to be a member of the interpack council—"

"The leader of the interpack council was contacted. He's sending a member to witness the challenge."

I collapsed onto the couch and clasped my hands to keep myself from trembling. It seemed they had made all the necessary preparations. I had waited too long to be honest with my father about the reason for my shifting problem, and now, when he needed me to be whole and strong, I'd be a liability instead.

"You don't need to worry, Samuel." My father squeezed my shoulder. "I'm stronger than Dirk Keller in both forms. He won't beat me."

"I know." And I did know my father was a better, stronger wolf and man than Dirk Keller. There was no doubt. My fear stemmed from something else, something my father either never knew or had long since forgotten.

"We don't have much time," he said. "You need to tell me everything there is to know about an Alpha challenge."

Reminding myself he would win, so the cause for my concern would never come to pass, I drew in a deep breath and started explaining the rules of an Alpha challenge.

"You'll meet in the battle ring, which is nothing more than a ten-foot circle cleared in the woods. You'll both be in your human forms, but you shouldn't wear clothing because you'll be expected to shift and there will be no time to disrobe. The council member present will call a start to the battle and give you ten minutes to fight as men—hand-to-hand only, no weapons. When the time is up, he'll yell for you to shift, and no matter where you are in the battle, you both must stop and take your wolf forms. This will continue every ten minutes—man to wolf and back again. Failure to immediately shift into the necessary form or remain in the form during the allotted time is automatic cause for disqualification, so you need to pay attention to the council member's call."

I paused and looked at my father, wanting to make sure he understood the importance of this rule. Once he nodded, I continued.

"At any time during the battle, either of you can admit defeat and bring an immediate end to the fighting. You can also both agree to a draw. Short of that, the fight is to the death." I gulped. "Only one shifter will leave the ring alive."

"That's it?" my father asked. His shoulders relaxed and the lines in his forehead smoothed. "Don't look so worried, Samuel. At worst, I'll suffer a slight injury, but it'll be well worth that price to rid the Miancarem pack of Dirk Keller's brand of leadership."

"Beating Dirk Keller in the ring won't be enough for that, Dad," I whispered.

"What do you mean? You said if he gives up or dies in the ring, I win." He narrowed his eyes. "He started this, but I plan to finish it once and for all. I won't agree to a draw."

"I understand. But besting Dirk in the challenge means you keep your position as Alpha of Yafenack, not that you gain control of Miancarem." I paused and, knowing we were limited on time, tried to explain in easy-to-understand terms the complex rules our ancestors created. "Think about a regular Alpha challenge where a pack member seeks to take over as Alpha. When the Alpha beats him, he retains his position, but there is no other prize. Well, he can banish the challenger's family from the pack, but that can be done by an Alpha at any time anyway, so it isn't anything—"

"Samuel," my father said, sounding tense. "If it isn't relevant to today's challenge, let's skip the lesson for now."

"Right. Yes." I nodded. "Like I was saying, the winner of an Alpha challenge traditionally gets to be Alpha. That's it. Now, in this case, there's a difference because there are two packs on the line, and so it might seem like the winner should get both packs, and that would be true except—" I took in a deep breath. "If there is a successor to the losing Alpha, he has the right to step into his role as soon as the current Alpha is no longer in place."

"I don't understand." My father furrowed his brow. "Once I beat Dirk, I don't take over the Miancarem pack?"

"It depends. When you defeat Dirk, you keep your position as Alpha of Yafenack. That's assured. And if there were no presumptive Alpha who could step up to lead Miancarem, you would fill that role as well." I licked my lips. "But as you know, Dirk has a son who is twenty-six, old enough to be Alpha."

"Yes?"

"That means Korban Keller has the right to be Alpha once his father steps down. His father's fight has nothing to do with his claim."

"But if I beat the Alpha, I win the right to lead his pack."

"If you beat the Alpha, you have a claim to lead his pack. But the presumptive Alpha has a claim too. That means when you beat Dirk there will be two claims to lead Miancarem. You can choose to walk away, keeping Yafenack and leaving Miancarem to Korban Keller."

I paused and tried to catch my breath.

"Or?" my father said impatiently. "There is an or, right?"

"Yes. In order to take over Miancarem, you'll either need Korban to acknowledge you as Alpha and give up his claim—"

"Nobody would ever do that."

"Or you'll need to fight him in the same way you fight his father." My chest ached and my stomach rolled over. "To the death."

"I see." He remained quiet for several long moments, his expression thoughtful. "And this fight will take place when?"

"Immediately after Dirk is defeated. If you seek to take over Dirk's pack, the presumptive Alpha will step into the ring and take over the battle. You'll continue from the exact same spot. You'll remain in the same form, and the council member will restart the clock from wherever it stopped."

"I've met Korban Keller on a couple of occasions, but I don't know him well."

"He's strong, Dad," I said hoarsely. "He's a strong wolf and a strong man."

I was having trouble thinking, sitting, breathing. To my horror, my eyes burned. I never cried. Never. And I wouldn't allow myself to start at that moment, even if my chest felt like it was ripping in two.

"So my choices will be leaving Miancarem to Dirk's son or battling him after I've been fighting with his father for who knows how long, even if I'm injured?"

I nodded, unable to formulate words.

"And if I lose?"

By that point, I was pretty sure he'd surmised the answer to that question. I cleared my throat. "The same rules apply. Korban can keep his pack, and if he wants Yafenack, the presumptive Alpha of our pack can step into the ring and continue the fight."

"You?"

"Yes."

No additional words needed to be said. We both knew I could never step into the ring, because once I shifted into my wolf form, I'd be unable to shift back in the time required. If I managed to shift back at all. Never in my entire life had I felt like more of a failure. I lowered my gaze in shame.

"It's okay, Samuel." My father patted my knee.

"I'm sorry." My voice shook, and I hated myself even more for the display of weakness.

"Don't be sorry for something you can't control." He cleared his throat. "Besides, it won't come up. If I'd wanted to be Alpha of Miancarem, I would have challenged Dirk long ago, right?"

That made sense. I raised my gaze hopefully.

"I'll beat Dirk in this challenge. And who knows? Maybe this newest Miancarem Alpha will be better than the others." He stood up. "Either way, it isn't our problem."

Those words were so unlike anything my father had ever said or taught me that I knew he didn't mean them. He wanted to help all shifters, not only those in our pack. That was part of what made him such a great Alpha. But Yafenack came first, and he wouldn't risk losing our pack to an outsider.

Defeating Dirk Keller was a sure thing. Beating a man nearly two decades his junior immediately after that battle wasn't as certain. I had no doubt my father would have tried it anyway and risked his life for the good of both packs. But to do that, he had to have faith in his backup—me. And we both knew that without being able to shift smoothly, I would fail the challenge.

CHAPTER 5

IN ORDER TO prevent a riot or unsanctioned fighting among the crowd, the interpack council had the right to limit the number of people who could attend a challenge. Heath Farbis, the council member sent to witness the battle between my father and Dirk Keller, limited the number of people to ten—five chosen by each Alpha. I would attend, of course. My brother and sister were too young to go. And despite the fact she would rather have been anywhere other than watching her husband fight, my mother insisted on coming to the battle.

"I'm the Alpha's mate. No matter what the writings say, my place is by his side," she said when I informed her that her presence wasn't required under pack law.

Figuring that was one of those unwritten cultural norms my father was forever trying to teach me, I accepted her explanation without further argument. I would have pushed harder if I had thought my father could be truly hurt in the battle. As it was, I knew Dirk Keller, and even though he was only a few years older than my father—forty-seven to my father's forty-four—he wasn't as tall, wasn't as strong, wasn't as smart, and wasn't as skilled. In other words, he was no match for my father.

After accounting for my mother and me, three spots remained for our side. My father filled them with his inner circle, the men who had been his friends since childhood and who still remained his closest confidants—Roger Huntsworth, Walter Clemson, and George Griffin. The battle ring was placed on the intersection between the two packs, with five feet in Miancarem's territory and the other five feet on Yafenack land. We arrived at sunset and remained beside the half of the ring on our territory, awaiting the moment when the sun completely left the sky and the battle would begin.

Everything was exactly as I'd read a challenge would be, with one exception: the presumptive Alpha of Miancarem wasn't there. Three times I'd counted the number of people on the Miancarem side, and three times I'd reached the number five despite the fact that Korban Keller wasn't present. His mother had passed when he was a child and his father had never remarried, so there wasn't a wife or other children to support the Alpha. My knowledge of the Keller clan was limited to information directly related to Korban, which meant I didn't know what other kin Dirk had. Based on scent, I suspected at least one of the five men he brought to the challenge was related to him. The scent was close enough to Dirk's that I suspected he was Dirk's brother.

But having a member of Dirk's family present didn't explain Korban's absence. His father was embarking on a fight to the death. That alone was reason for his attendance. Aside from that, he was the presumptive Alpha of the Miancarem pack, which meant he would have to step into the ring to defend his position when my father won the fight. If Korban was out of the picture, my father would be the only person with a claim to lead the Miancarem pack.

No matter how many times I rolled it over in my mind, I couldn't come up with a rational explanation for Korban to miss such an important event. I considered the possibility that he had taken ill, which made my chest tighten inexplicably, but I quickly regained my breath when I remembered that Dirk Keller was the one who had issued the challenge. There was nothing special about that crisp October evening, nothing that would warrant calling an immediate challenge unless all the parties were in optimal health. So surely Korban wasn't sick.

Certain he was on his way and would switch places with one of the other witnesses on the Miancarem side at any moment, I watched for him. Wondering about Korban Keller was an effective distraction while we stood and waited for the fight to start, but once the council member started talking, I turned my full attention to the battle.

"We're here tonight because the Alpha of the Miancarem pack, Dirk Keller, challenged the Alpha of the Yafenack pack, Tom Goodwin. The battle will start in your human forms and last ten minutes before switching to your wolf forms. This will continue every ten minutes. I will give you a warning thirty seconds in advance of the ten-minute mark, at which point you can shift forms. I will notify you again at the ten-minute mark and then when thirty seconds have passed. If you fail to complete your shift by thirty seconds after the ten-minute mark, you will be automatically disqualified and lose the challenge." Heath Farbis paused and looked at my father and Dirk before continuing. "You must remain completely inside the ring at all times. If you find any part of your body outside the ring, you must immediately return to the ring or you will be disqualified. Are there any questions before we begin?"

No Alpha with an ounce of intelligence would have shown up to the challenge without knowing the basic rules. Asking a question at that point would have shown weakness, which neither challenger could risk, so it was no surprise that both Dirk and my father remained quiet. I wasn't worried. The council member's explanation matched my understanding of the rules surrounding a challenge, and so, if nothing else, I had prepared my father well on that front.

"With no questions spoken, we're ready to begin." The council member stretched his arm out and gestured to the circle. "Both challengers may now enter the ring."

My father stripped out of his clothes and stepped over the rocks delineating the battle ring. He remained on the Yafenack side and looked his competitor over. Dirk Keller did the same on the Miancarem side. Comparing the two men based on their physical appearances made me wonder how Dirk could think he stood a chance against my taller, stronger father. The people around me relaxed, no doubt having made the same assessment and feeling confident our Alpha would prevail.

"The first ten-minute round starts...now!" Heath Farbis said.

Knowing the rules of a challenge didn't mean I had any idea how the people in the ring would actually proceed. I hadn't had enough time to give it much thought, so I didn't have a vision in my head of how the fight would go minute to minute, but I was surprised by the mild reaction at the beginning. It was somewhat anticlimactic, hearing the shout that signaled the start of the most important event I would ever witness and then...nothing.

My father and Dirk continued staring at one another, their expressions unchanged. Neither man leaped forward or growled; neither made a move to get closer to the other. Instead, they remained deathly quiet and slowly circled the ring, their gazes locked together.

"He's going to be okay," my mother whispered to nobody in particular.

"Yes," I replied distractedly as I tried to make sense of what I was seeing.

My father wasn't violent, short-tempered, or easy to inflame. Because of that, quietly watching Dirk rather than jumping into combat made sense. What I couldn't understand was Dirk's reaction.

For years Dirk Keller had been quick to blame my father for the problems he had created within his own pack. He was disrespectful and thoughtless. Plus, he had issued the challenge. With what I knew about Dirk, I would have expected him to throw the first punch or least the first verbal barb.

And yet he didn't do either of those things. The clock ticked and nobody got within fist's reach of each other. I wasn't the only person confused by the direction the battle was taking. The brush on the forest floor rustled as the men around me squirmed uncomfortably. One of them whispered, "What are they doing?" and I was certain the others were wondering the same thing.

We weren't the only ones who recognized the oddness of the situation. My father's expression had gone from intense to confused. He was still watching Dirk, still holding a stance ready to defend any attack, but his eyebrows were knitted slightly closer together, his lips were pressed a smidge tighter, and his head was tilted a hair to the side.

Something wasn't right. I couldn't put my finger on what it was, but Dirk's behavior was off. He wasn't acting like himself or even like what I would have expected of any Alpha who issued a challenge. I wondered if he was employing a complex fighting strategy and internally kicked myself for never having thought of studying something like that. An Alpha challenge was unheard of in modern times, but that wasn't an excuse for being unprepared. I had learned all aspects of shifter culture and rules; I should have also taken the time to learn about the best way to implement them.

I was about thigh-deep in internal reprimands when sudden movement in the ring stole my focus. My father was rushing across the circle, aiming for Dirk. Though I hadn't expected that turn of events, I sighed in relief, certain it meant he had figured out Dirk's strategy even when I couldn't.

From the first strike, there was no doubt about which shifter was stronger. Dirk widened his eyes in surprise and threw up his hands in an attempt to defend himself, but he didn't succeed. My father pushed past his outstretched arms, landed a perfect right hook on his jaw, and then grasped his throat, squeezing tightly as he raised the weaker man off the ground.

His face turning darker, Dirk clawed at my father's arms and wrists, trying to loosen the grip cutting off his air supply. He flailed his legs, making occasional contact with my father's thighs and knees. The kicks did nothing but elicit an occasional grunt from my father. He held firm, occasionally shaking the other Alpha like he would an animal he hunted in wolf form.

Just as Dirk was about to crumple into unconsciousness, he seemed to gather all his remaining strength, and then he swung hard. I doubted he had the skill or wherewithal to aim well, but he got lucky and hit my father directly on his throat. Whether it was the unexpected pain or having his breath cut off, I didn't know, but my father must have relaxed his grip because Dirk managed to slip through his fingers.

After landing on the ground, the man gasped for air for less than a second before he shook his head, blinked rapidly, and darted his gaze around. My father coughed for a few moments, and that was all the time Dirk needed to identify the Miancarem half of the circle. He started scurrying backward, his backside dragging on the leaf-covered ground.

"Thirty seconds before the ten-minute mark," the council member said, pitching his voice to ensure he'd be heard.

My father wasted no time, immediately shifting into his wolf form. I would have expected Dirk to do the same, but instead, he continued dragging himself farther toward the edge of the ring, where his pack members were crouched low to the ground. I hoped he was trying to get away and that he wouldn't stop until he left the ring entirely, which would disqualify him and end the battle without my father having to live with the guilt of killing him. It would be the perfect outcome.

"Ten minutes," the council member said. "You must shift into your wolf form immediately."

Dirk still hadn't shifted. He had thirty seconds left before he'd be disqualified for an entirely different reason than leaving the battle ring. He had reached the edge of the ring, and I was hopeful he would cross over, but suddenly he stopped, presumably remembering his pride and changing his mind.

Not wasting any time, my father leaped forward. He landed on top of Dirk just as the man rolled over onto his back. They scuffled, and then Dirk shifted into his wolf form with only a few seconds to spare. Though he wouldn't be disqualified, I was certain it was too late for him to win the challenge or stay alive because my father's jaw was open and he closed it over Dirk's throat.

They were on the side of the ring opposite me, so despite the moon shining down on us and my shifter vision, I couldn't see what happened next. One second I was waiting to see blood gush from Dirk's throat, and the next my father was tumbling to the ground. He climbed to his feet, but it was awkward at best. I leaned forward and squinted, trying to identify an injury I hadn't seen being inflicted.

Still recovering from the beating my father had given him, Dirk was slow, but he managed to jump onto my father, claws and teeth bared. It was hard to follow anything after that as the two wolves rolled together without grace—growling, snapping, and clawing. The scent of blood was heavy in the air, and when I saw my father's light brown fur darkening, I truly worried for the first time during the battle.

"What's going on?" one of our pack members murmured. "Tom doesn't fight like this."

Though I hadn't seen my father fight often, I understood what he meant. My father normally had more finesse and control. The wolf we were watching had neither. He seemed unable to get his bearings; his coordination was nonexistent, and whatever strategy I'd thought he was employing was gone. As the minutes ticked by, my father's bites and swipes went from spasmodic to ill-timed, until to my horror, they stopped altogether.

"Tom!"

"Alpha!"

The shouts around me sounded like they were coming from far away as I tried to reconcile what my eyes were seeing with the only outcome I had thought possible.

"No!" my mother cried out.

Why wasn't he moving? Why was the ground turning red underneath him?

Time stopped. Sounds stopped. Everything stopped while I watched the life leach from my father's body.

Someone was talking. It took me a few moments to realize it was the council member, and even then I couldn't make out his words. My father's friends stepped into the ring and lifted his body from the ground. I looked around and saw my mother, tears streaming down her face as she watched her husband's corpse being carried to her.

"Samuel Goodwin, you need to respond!"

My name being shouted finally got my attention. I blinked at the council member.

"What?" I croaked.

"Dirk Keller won the challenge," Heath Farbis said, and I had the sense he was repeating words I had missed. "That means he retains his position in the Miancarem pack and he has a claim to the Yafenack pack. As the presumptive Alpha of the Yafenack pack, you have the right to fight for your position. What do you choose?"

I was trying to think my way through the fog in my brain to answer his question when Dirk suddenly yelled, "But I won! Both packs are mine."

Why was he in human form? When had he shifted?

"Alpha, control yourself," the council member snapped. "As I just explained to you, winning the challenge means you have a claim to the Yafenack pack. If there is another with a claim present, which there is, he has the right to fight for control just as you do."

Though his face was full of rage and he shook with barely contained fury, Dirk managed to nod. "Fine! I will call for a challenge when—"

"No." The council member shook his head. "The rules are clear. The battle continues until all shifters with a claim to the Alpha position have relinquished their claims or lost the battle. You will have no other opportunity to challenge the Yafenack pack if you forfeit now."

"What does that mean?" Dirk said as he turned to his pack members. "Did you know about this?"

The panicked mumbling, wide eyes, and shaking heads answered that question.

And so did the council member. "It means if you want to take over as Alpha of the Yafenack pack, you must defeat all those with a claim to the position." He pointed at me. "Samuel Goodwin is twenty-three years old and the presumptive Alpha of the pack. He has a claim, which means he can step into the challenge where his father left off—with one minute left as a wolf. You will then both shift into your human forms for ten minutes and so on and so forth. You already heard the rules of battle, Alpha. I shouldn't have to repeat them." The man had clearly lost his patience.

I, on the other hand, was finally starting to regain my mind. My Alpha was dead. My father was dead.

"But I've already been battling and he hasn't," Dirk said, as if we hadn't all been present for it. "That isn't fair."

I would have laughed at him for sounding like a whiney child if I had the ability, but I doubted I would ever laugh again.

"You called this challenge and insisted it happen at the earliest allowable time, Alpha." The council member's lips were thin white lines. "The council dropped everything to accommodate your demand. Perhaps you should have thought to learn more about the rules." He waved his hand at the Miancarem witnesses. "For example, I understood your pack to have a presumptive Alpha as well, but I see he isn't here."

"I'm still the Alpha of my pack!" Dirk bellowed.

"For now, yes." The council member smirked before turning to me, his gaze softening. "Samuel Goodwin, do you wish to meet the challenge of your claim to the Yafenack pack?"

The fate of my pack rested with me. No matter what happened in that ring, walking away from the challenge and abandoning my pack was not an option. My father raised me with honor.

"Yes," I said, trying to put every ounce of strength I didn't have into my voice.

My mother cried out, her voice anguished, but she didn't argue.

"Mom," I said. "You don't need to stay."

"I'm staying." Her eyes were red, her face was wet, but her voice was firm.

I suddenly flashed back to her words over the years, explaining that despite not being an Alpha herself, she understood the responsibilities we had. For the first time, I grasped the truth of her statement. Her husband's body was not yet cold, and still she stood and waited for her eldest son to walk into battle.

"I'm sorry," I said, my gaze locked with hers.

A soft nod was the only response she was capable of giving me, but I knew she understood. Being the only person present with complete knowledge of my shifting issue, she was the only one who truly grasped what was about to happen.

"Enter the ring in your wolf forms and wait for my command," the council member said. "You will continue the battle just as it ended—with fifty seconds left. I will notify you at the thirty-second mark and again when the time ends."

I had less than a minute as a wolf to kill Dirk. After that, I silently prayed my body would heel to my command for the first time in years and shift. Otherwise, I would be disqualified and all would be lost.

I closed my eyes, inhaled deeply, and then began to methodically remove my clothing. I heard Dirk grumbling but I ignored him and turned my focus inward, using all the failed strategies I'd tried over the past few years to control my shift. When I was finally undressed, I folded my things, stacked them neatly, and tucked them behind a nearby tree. Then I dropped to the ground and let my wolf free.

After so long being caged, it felt wonderful to be in my wolf skin. But with the pain in my heart and the fear in my gut, I couldn't revel in it. Instead, I walked into the ring and waited for the council member to give me permission to rip out the throat of the man who had taken my father from me.

For a moment, I thought I would defeat Dirk without satisfying my need for vengeance. Rather than shift when he was told, Dirk continued arguing with the council member, insisting he had already won the challenge and both packs were his. But when he was told in no uncertain terms that he was wrong, that the rules had been written for generations, and that he would be disqualified if he didn't step into the ring, Dirk finally complied.

Time moved in slow motion after that.

Dirk lowered his bruised and battered body to the ground and took his wolf form.

An image of Korban Keller's white wolf shot into my brain, and I thought of how different they looked from one another. Dirk had none of Korban's beauty or grace. Plus their eyes—Dirk didn't have those mesmerizing navy eyes.

The council member shouted for us to begin.

Dirk turned tail and ran.

I bared my teeth and pounced, landing exactly where I'd aimed— on top of the shifter I planned to kill.

Dirk whined and wriggled, trying to get free.

I bit his back, his shoulders, his nape, trying to reach around his body to his throat and reveling in the coppery taste filling my mouth as I gouged and wounded him.

There was shouting and chaos all around me, demands that we shift back to our human forms. I ignored them at first, but when Dirk somehow managed to take his human skin and lay beneath me with rips over most of his body, I tried to shift.

"Ten more seconds," the council member yelled, and even through the fog, I knew that was an extra warning, one to which I wasn't entitled. "You must shift or be disqualified, Samuel!"

But I couldn't shift. No matter how hard I tried, my wolf wouldn't let go. And when time ran out, I was suddenly under attack, not by the unconscious man beneath me, but by his witnesses. They had the right, I knew, to keep me away from their Alpha. The challenge was over. I had failed.

With my entire being drenched in sorrow and shame, I fought my way free of the Miancarem shifters surrounding me and ran into the woods. I didn't know where I was going. It didn't matter. I had failed the challenge, failed my father, and failed my pack.

My howl echoed off the trees as I did the only thing I could. I ran.

CHAPTER 6

ALTHOUGH I was more in touch with my base instincts as an animal than I was as a man, I still had the same memories, the same intellect, and the same knowledge. So as I raced through the woods, I was keenly aware of my loss and my failure. A part of me knew I had to shift back eventually, because my mother would be worried and she'd need me to be strong for her and the rest of the family. But I doubted that would be possible, doubted I'd be able to control my shift enough to take my human form.

Deep down, I was grateful. Maybe if I stayed in my wolf form long enough, everyone would forget about me and I could forget about them, forget about my human half, forget about seeing my father's blood spill on the forest floor. With my birthright to become Alpha of the Yafenack pack gone, I could live out my days in my animal form doing what came so naturally and easily instead of suffering through the discomfort that inevitably came when I tried to fit in with other people.

Unable to think clearly enough to choose a destination, I wandered aimlessly and lost track of time. I didn't know where I was or the exact hour, but the orange glow of the sun was just beginning to peek over the horizon when I felt a call, an urge, a need to move in a certain direction. Too tired to resist it, I followed my gut and walked through the trees and brush, over a few hills and valleys, and before I knew it, I started recognizing things—scents at first, and then the landscape.

I was near the scene of the challenge.

I had to stop. I had to turn around. I had to run.

But when I tried, the call within me got louder, more insistent, until I couldn't deny it, and despite the pain in my chest, I increased my pace and ran toward the battle ring. The other shifters had long since left, so the place that would haunt me for all of time was quiet and deserted; the only signs of what had taken place there were the rocks and the blood-spattered brush.

For a few moments, all I could do was stare and whimper.

Why was I there? Why couldn't I leave?

Somehow my questions were answered within my head. I needed to go look at the brush next to the rocks that formed the edge of the ring a few feet in front of me. Though I didn't know what I was looking for, I moved forward anyway.

The scents of the shifters who had witnessed the battle were still thick in the air, but my father's blood was the only smell I could focus on. Not being an emotional person, I rarely felt pain unless it was physical, and even when I did, the ache never penetrated deeper than a surface level. But as I walked over that land, I ached all the way through my core. Still, I took one step at a time, following the voice inside urging me to find something.

Even with the sun rising in the sky and light filtering in through the trees, I didn't see it at first because it was hidden under leaves and pine needles. But then I moved, altering the angle of my gaze, and I noticed a bright reflection. It lasted no longer than a second, but that was enough. Tilting my head to the side, I moved closer, focused on the object partially buried between rocks and brush, and tried to identify it.

I was about to poke it with my muzzle when that internal voice told me to stop, not to touch. Once again, I obeyed without hesitation and halted where I stood. It didn't take long for me to recognize the object, even without touching it—a syringe. There was a syringe in the battle ring. But why?

Blinking, I looked back over one shoulder and then the other, trying to correlate the location of the syringe to where every step of the battle had taken place. It was on the Miancarem side; that much I knew. I closed my eyes and thought back to when my father pounced and took hold of Dirk's neck. That had been at a spot further within the ring and behind me. After that, Dirk had crawled away, toward his pack members, who had been standing...

My eyes flew open. There. I looked at the syringe. They had been standing just on the other side of the rocks, and Dirk had gone to that very spot. I was sure of it. That was where my father landed on him in his wolf form, ready to tear out his throat before everything fell apart.

It hadn't made sense, the way my father suddenly lost control over the fight, the way he had moved with no coordination and fought with no grace. It wasn't like him and, when I thought about it, it had come out of nowhere. One moment he was pure strength and power, and the next he was stumbling and awkward. Had someone drugged him? Was that why there was a syringe lying in the brush?

Once again, I darted toward the offending object and once again the voice inside told me to stop. I shivered with exhaustion, sorrow, and rage, my mind a jumble of thoughts. I had to do something, but figuring out what was too difficult in that moment. And then, like a beam of clarity, I knew what I had to do.

I would call the interpack council and ask them to send a witness to the battle ring so he could see the syringe for himself. That would prove Dirk Keller had drugged my father and killed him without honor and outside of pack law. It wouldn't return our Alpha to us, but at least my pack would be free of Dirk.

With a plan in place, I was calmer, more at peace. I would find a phone, call the council, and vindicate my father. Almost immediately, I remembered I had left my clothing behind a tree. My cell phone had been in my pocket, so unless someone had thought to take my clothes home—which was unlikely given everything else my pack had been dealing with after the challenge—it would still be there.

Within moments, I had located the right tree and found my clothing. The next step would be more difficult—to use a cell phone, I had to shift into my human form.

Focusing on the man within, I tried to change into my human skin over and over again, failing each time. Seconds turned to minutes, the sun rose higher in the sky, and still I remained in my wolf form. Howling in frustration at my failure, I began losing hope. But then a calmness filled me, soothing my tense muscles, whispering soft sounds in my mind and slowly, gently coaxing my body through the shift.

Once I was in my human form, I sprang into action. I grabbed for my phone and called the interpack council leader first. There was no answer, but I left an urgent message, deciding I'd give him ten minutes to call back before ringing him again. Thankfully it didn't take him that long. I'd had just enough time to throw on my clothes and tie my shoes when my phone rang.

My words were short, but to the point. "I have reason to believe Dirk Keller violated the rules of the challenge and drugged my father. Please send a council member to collect the proof. I'm at the battle ring, waiting."

The urge to destroy the instrument used to kill my father was strong, so I forced myself to stay on the other side of the ring. Too ramped up to sit or think, I paced back and forth with my gaze locked on the syringe.

I scented the council members before I saw them—Heath Farbis, who had witnessed the battle, and a man who smelled vaguely familiar from the times I'd accompanied my father to interpack meetings, but not familiar enough that I could remember his name. Though I wasn't aware of the time, it felt like not long had passed since my phone call, making me wonder how they'd arrived so soon. My focus didn't remain on that question, however. My only goal was to protect my pack from Dirk Keller and seek retribution for my father's death.

"Samuel Goodwin," the man I didn't recognize said as he reached his hand out to me. "I'm Anthony Lang, and you already know Heath Farbis."

My patience, which was limited on the best of days, was nonexistent by that point. Between the sleep deprivation, stress, and sorrow, I felt like a string wound so tight it would snap at any moment. Despite that, I forced myself to take his hand and shake it. My father would have expected me to show respect, and I would make him proud in whatever way I could, even after his death. A sharp pain almost brought me to my knees at that reminder, but I managed to remain upright, my back straight and shoulders squared.

"Thank you for coming." I paused and considered whether that was enough polite conversation and I could move on to what mattered.

Thankfully, Heath was of a like mind. "The message we received said you had reason to believe Dirk Keller cheated during the challenge. Tell us what you know."

Reading people had never been my strong suit, but I didn't hear any animosity or disbelief in his tone. I hoped that meant they would take my discovery seriously.

"I returned here..." I faltered midsentence, unsure of the exact time of my return or even how long I'd been waiting for them. Shaking my head in the hopes of clearing away distractions, I took in a deep breath and tried again. "I returned here at sunrise, shortly before I called the interpack council leader. My gut told me something was wrong and I had to return to the battle ring to find it." That was perhaps not the most accurate description of the voice I'd heard in my head, leading me to the ring, to the syringe, and through my shift, but it was the clearest way I could explain it. "I didn't see it at first, but then the sun bounced off it and"—I pointed toward the syringe on the opposite side of the circle—"I realized what it was."

Both men squinted in the direction I was pointing.

"It's a syringe," I said, my voice starting to shake. "There's a syringe buried in the brush, right next to the rocks. That's the spot where—"

"That's where Dirk Keller shifted," Heath said as he started walking toward the syringe. Anthony followed him. "He was in his human form, Tom Goodwin had just shifted into his wolf skin, and they had started wrestling." Heath squatted next to the syringe and then twisted his head around and looked up at Anthony. "That was when control of the battle changed hands."

With a sharp nod, Anthony joined him lower to the ground. "You said you found this here?" he asked without looking at me.

"Yes." I gulped and cleared my throat, trying to make my voice sound strong. "I didn't touch it."

Another nod from Anthony, and then he looked at Heath. "Do you think Dirk Keller will admit to drugging his challenger once he's faced with the proof?"

I scoffed, which would have been rude if Heath hadn't done the same.

"No," Heath said with a snarl. "I don't believe Alpha Keller will take responsibility for anything."

"Then we'll need to prove this syringe was used on Alpha Goodwin and that whatever it contains harmed him during the challenge." He removed a handkerchief from his pocket and wrapped it around the syringe.

"How will you do that?" I asked.

"There's a healer in another pack. He's had...extensive training. I spoke with him on the way here, and he can make the determination. I'll bring him the syringe and I'll ask your pack healer to draw a blood sample from your father's body. That's all he said he'd need."

Something didn't make sense about his statement, but I was too tired and worried to figure out what it was.

For the first time, Anthony looked me in the eyes. "I'm sorry about your loss, Samuel. Your father was a good Alpha. I had great respect for him."

"Thank you." I had to focus on the pack; it's what my father would have done. "What about my pack?"

"Your pack?"

I squared my shoulders. "Yes. With my father gone, I am now the Alpha of the Yafenack pack."

"You were disqualified, Samuel," Heath said. "I realize the emotions surrounding your father's death made it difficult for you to focus and shift during the required time, but—"

Grateful he didn't realize the real reason I hadn't shifted, I felt stronger, more able to advocate for my pack. "Dirk Keller violated the rules of the challenge before I entered the ring. That means he was disqualified first." And perhaps there was a greater penalty due to him; I'd research the writings when I got home and figure out if there was any information I could use to protect my pack from Dirk and avenge my father.

Anthony and Heath exchanged uncomfortable looks. "I've never had an issue like this arise," Anthony said.

"I haven't either," Heath said.

They were both silent, and then Anthony said, "The healer will test the syringe, and then we'll discuss this matter with the interpack council."

"And until then?" I pushed.

They looked at each other again and, after a pause, Heath turned to me. "You will serve as Alpha of the Yafenack pack for now. We will revisit this once we have more information."

I nodded and tried to feel grateful, but all I could feel was pain over the loss of my father, fear that my shifting issue would prevent me from protecting my pack, and, despite my attempt to stop thinking about Korban Keller, worry about why he had missed the challenge.

CHAPTER 7

BETWEEN THE drive to the gathering, being surrounded by people while I tried and failed to find someone I could tie with, the drive back to Yafenack, the challenge, the night wandering through the woods, and the morning spent with the interpack council members, I hadn't slept in more than three days. And they'd been stressful, busy days. So by the time I got home after accompanying Heath Farbis and Anthony Lang to obtain a sample of my father's blood, I was barely able to stay upright.

I had planned to go straight to my room, bathe, and then sleep. But somehow I'd ended up leaning against the wall next to the front door, my eyes closed and my muscles tense. I had no idea how long I'd been there when I heard my mother's voice.

"Samuel! Thank goodness you're all right."

"I'm sorry," I said immediately. Then, after swallowing hard, I opened my eyes and, difficult though it was, looked her straight in the face. Her skin was pale, her hair disheveled, and her eyes red-rimmed. "I'm so sorry. I know I failed him, failed the pack, but I'll find a way to fix it. I'll avenge him. I'll—"

"Shhhh." My mother walked right up and hugged me. She'd done that more frequently than everyone else I knew combined, but I still stiffened at the feel of arms around me, still felt awkward being touched, and still didn't know how I was supposed to respond or what I was supposed to do with my hands or how long I'd have to endure it before I stepped away. "It isn't your fault, Samuel. None of it is your fault," she whispered.

That wasn't true. I should have noticed something was wrong during the fight. My father wasn't acting right, and yet I stood by and did nothing. And then there was my shift—what kind of Alpha couldn't control his shift? I should have been honest with my father. He could have helped me before it was too late, but I had let my pride rule me and take away any chance I had of fixing my problem and doing the one thing I'd trained for my entire life—leading my pack.

"We've been waiting for you," my mother said. She hadn't yet stepped away, and I felt itchy and sweaty having a body so close to mine. "We're packed and I have bags and boxes ready for you."

When I didn't respond, she finally released me and moved back. I sighed in relief.

"I would have packed for you," she said. "But I didn't think you'd want me in your room, going through your things."

I flinched at the mere thought of anyone else in my personal space, touching my clothes, my books, my computer, moving things around. "You're right. I can pack my own..." My brain caught up to the conversation, and I furrowed my brow in confusion. "Why are we packing?"

"We can't stay here, Samuel. I will not give Dirk Keller the opportunity to harass us or speak ill of your father in front of your sister and brother." Her voice shook with animosity, which was out of character but understandable given the circumstances. "We're leaving Yafenack. I've already called and gotten permission for us to join the Etzgadol pack. The Harrisons will house us right away. I want us out of this house and off pack lands before Dirk Keller arrives."

"Dirk Keller isn't coming here!"

"What do you mean?" she asked in confusion. "He might not live here, but he will come and go as he pleases. He's the Al—" She lost her breath and whimpered midword.

I understood how difficult it was to call someone other than my father Alpha. Especially if that someone was a murdering scoundrel. And it wouldn't happen. Not while I still had a breath left in my—admittedly traitorous—body.

"No, he isn't," I growled. "I am Alpha of this pack and I will not let Dirk Keller step foot on our land. He will pay for what he did to my father."

After looking at me in concern, my mother drew in a deep breath and, with her voice calm and her expression sympathetic, said, "Samuel, you were disqualified during the challenge. That means you lost."

I winced in response to the reminder of my failure, but I didn't let it stop me from keeping my focus. "I discovered a syringe in the battle ring this morning, and I believe it'll prove Dirk Keller violated the rules during the challenge and poisoned Dad. I've already met with representatives from the interpack council, and they're testing it to confirm my theory. They agreed I'm Alpha of the Yafenack pack for now, not Dirk Keller."

"Poisoned?" she gasped.

"They haven't tested the syringe yet, but yes."

"That's why he was moving so strangely after he shifted."

She was talking to herself, not to me, so I didn't respond.

"How... Why..." She choked on her words and shivered.

Though I wanted to help, I wasn't sure what to say or do, so I stayed perfectly still and waited until she composed herself. My mother was strong, so it didn't take long.

"You're sure?" she asked me.

I nodded, my gut telling me that was exactly what had happened.

"Then Dirk Keller won't be Alpha of our pack." She swallowed hard. "That's good. I'm glad." She closed her eyes and breathed in deeply before opening her eyes again. "Everything is ready except your things, Samuel. Go fill your bags and then we can leave."

Furrowing my brow in confusion, I said, "But we don't need to leave. Dirk Keller won't be Alpha."

"That's true, but someone will."

I was missing something, I realized, but I didn't know what it was.

"I'm Alpha," I said, knowing I was repeating myself. "The council members said they'd test the syringe and—"

"Samuel." My mother stepped close to me again and cupped my cheek.

It wasn't easy, but I forced myself not to pull away from her touch.

"You know I love you," she said.

"Yes." She had told me all my life. I knew.

"If you try to remain Alpha of this pack, you'll have to shift. People will notice if you don't, and then you'll be challenged."

She was right. I had no doubt that was exactly what would happen. I couldn't be Alpha, despite the fact that was all I'd ever wanted to be. But I could still care for the pack in the way an Alpha should. "It's my duty to make sure everything is resolved with Dirk and the pack is in good hands."

"Dirk Keller won't take this lying down. And if he poisoned your father in front of a council member, he has no limit." Her voice broke as she added, "He'll hurt you."

It was possible. But that didn't change my duty.

"For as long as I'm Alpha, my duty is to protect the pack. The pack comes first."

We'd both heard my father say those words time and again. She couldn't argue about it with me. And she didn't.

"I don't want Eddie and Jen to see the fallout. I don't want them hurt. And living here"—she moved her hand around, gesturing to our home—"without your father and someone else as Alpha will hurt all of us."

She was right. Nothing would ever be the same again, and my brother and sister should be shielded as much as possible.

"I agree," I said. "You should take them to Etzgadol."

"And what about you?"

"The pack needs me. I have to put the pack before myself."

Swallowing hard, she nodded. "But after things are resolved with the council, you'll join us?"

My wolf form was so overpowering, I was amazed I'd been able to shift back into my human form that day. It was more difficult than ever to keep my wolf at bay. The next time that part of me took over could very well be the last. But I would persevere long enough to avenge my father and ensure the security of my pack.

"Yes," I said.

Lying wasn't something my father condoned, but I hoped he would have agreed with my decision to spare my mother's feelings in that moment. Besides, after my display in the battle ring, we both knew I'd likely never see her again, at least not in human form.

Though she looked sad, my mother smiled and said, "I'll get your brother and sister so they can say goodbye to you before we leave."

My grandfather and his father had built our house with their own hands. My mother had spent years updating it after my father took over as Alpha. My siblings and I had been born there. And because of Dirk Keller, it would no longer be home to the Goodwins.

The council members had said it would take several days to determine the contents of the syringe and compare it to my father's blood. I had an idea of how to punish Dirk Keller, but I would spend that time refreshing my already solid knowledge of shifter rules to ensure justice would be served and he would suffer more than the loss of the challenge. Dirk Keller would regret what he did; he would beg for mercy, and then he would die.

Ten days had passed, and I hadn't heard from the interpack council. I had spent the time researching the old texts to confirm my memory of the rules and reassuring the pack that they were safe, that their lives would not change, and that I would protect them. The research and packing was easy. Getting the pack members to fully trust me was not.

After years of being groomed to lead them, they still weren't completely comfortable around me. My father used to say it was because I wasn't completely comfortable around them, which was true. But then, I wasn't completely comfortable around anybody, and I didn't see why that had any bearing on my ability to protect the members and ensure the safety and prosperity of the pack.

Less than two weeks as their leader and I realized my father was right. Being strong, knowledgeable, and dedicated wasn't enough. The pack members didn't like me, and that created anxiety and discord. As it was, the main reason I received even grudging respect was my plan to avenge my father's death. The pack members loved him, and knowing I would punish the man who took him from them went a long way toward earning their respect.

Already, I'd heard grumblings about my not being the right person to lead the pack, and they didn't even know about my shifting problem. If that information got out, Rick Collins—the man who had been staring me down at every opportunity and making no secret about his opinion that he'd be a better Alpha—would gain the support of the entire pack, including those people who were loyal to my family.

I wouldn't have minded as much if I'd thought Rick would make a good Alpha, but I didn't. Knowing I would ultimately have to walk away from my pack didn't change my duty to ensure they had a strong leader, and that would not be Rick. Once I finished dealing with Dirk Keller and eliminating the threat from outside our pack, I'd focus on finding the best leader from within our pack to take my spot.

My only hope was that I'd be able to keep my wolf caged that long. As it was, my skin felt hot and tight, I was having trouble sleeping and regulating my body temperature, and several times a day, I had to stand perfectly still and breathe deeply to keep myself from spontaneously shifting.

Pack members had been stopping by the house in a fairly steady stream—some to give their condolences, some to seek assistance from their Alpha, and others, I suspected, to test me to see if I was up to the job. So when the doorbell rang on Thursday afternoon, I assumed it was a member of my pack. When I reached the door, I was able to smell the man on the other side and I realized my wait was over.

"Anthony Lang," I said as I opened the door. "I wasn't expecting you."

"Hello, Samuel." He reached his hand out to me and I shook it. "I told you I'd be back as soon as we received the results from the tests on the syringe."

"Yes, but I thought you'd call first."

When he frowned, I realized my mistake. I hadn't invited him in and I'd expected him to utilize human technology. Both things probably fell under my father's definition of rude. I could be persuaded to agree about the former, but the latter was ridiculous.

It was neither the time nor the place for that debate, though, so I changed course and said, "Thank you for traveling all this way. Come in." I cleared my throat and stepped back, leaving room for him to enter the house, and then, as an afterthought, said, "Please."

"Thank you." Anthony walked into the entryway and looked around. "Is your mother here? My wife asked me to pass along her regards and condolences."

"No. My mother moved after…" I swallowed hard. "My mother, brother, and sister have joined the Etzgadol pack. It was too difficult to stay here."

"Oh." Anthony jerked back. "I had no idea. I'm surprised Zev Hassick didn't mention it."

Though I was new to the position of Alpha, I was not new to all it entailed. My father had kept me by his side for all decisions, large and small. There was no requirement—written or unwritten—to notify the interpack council when a family joined a pack. I would have asked Anthony for clarification in order to expand my knowledge base and ensure I acted appropriately as Alpha when the next family joined the Yafenack pack, but my wolf was scratching at me to get out with such desperation I doubted I'd remain Alpha long enough to welcome a new family to my pack.

"I'll pass on your wife's regards," I said, internally patting myself on the back for being polite. "Would you like to sit down?" That was two for two.

"Yes. That's a good idea."

I led Anthony to the living room, waited for him to take a seat on the sofa, and then settled into one of the armchairs.

"What did you find out?" I asked when he didn't speak right away. I had been polite, invited him in, and made small talk. It was time to get down to business.

"You were right about the syringe," he said. "It contained a drug called quinuclidinyl benzilate, which is used to incapacitate people. Your father had it in his system."

Hearing the confirmation of how my father died took my breath away, but only for a moment. That was what I had expected to hear, what I had been preparing to hear, and I was ready.

"Dirk Keller killed my father, which means—"

"We don't know that exactly," Anthony said. "There is no way to confirm who injected your father unless a witness steps forward, which isn't likely because the poisoning took place on the Miancarem side of the battle ring."

Rage filled me. Jumping to my feet, I shouted, "Are you disputing Dirk's violation of the—"

"No." Anthony held up his hand in a placating gesture. "Regardless of who handled the syringe, there is no way Dirk Keller didn't see what happened. Heath was very clear about where they were positioned, and it was impossible for Dirk to have missed it. Besides, he is responsible for his witnesses."

My rage ebbed, and my heart slowed so blood was no longer pounding in my ears. "Dirk Keller violated the rules of the challenge," I said.

"Yes." Anthony nodded. "His claim to lead the Yafenack pack is void. Heath Farbis is delivering the news now. That leaves you as the only shifter with a claim to the pack, so you will remain Alpha."

That explained why Anthony had come alone. I had expected the council member who had witnessed the battle to join him. Regardless, I had all the information I needed to move forward with my plan.

"On behalf of the Yafenack pack, I call for retribution." I spoke the words as they were written in the texts.

"Retribution?" Anthony furrowed his brow. "As I said, you will remain Alpha of the Yafenack pack."

"I am the only person with a valid claim to the position. That doesn't constitute retribution."

"What do you mean?" Anthony asked.

I took in a breath, mentally went over what I'd read, and then sat down, trying to remain calm. "Our Alpha was killed outside of pack rules, and the killing was sanctioned by another Alpha. As such, the Yafenack pack is entitled to retribution."

"Retri—" Anthony gasped midword. "You're calling for a tribute?"

"Yes. It's our right."

"In ancient times, yes, but it isn't done now."

"Neither is a challenge to the death," I growled. "But Dirk Keller insisted on it. He called on the old rules, demanded we adhere to them, and we complied." I squeezed my fists and forced myself to be clear and professional. I knew the rules better than anybody, and the texts were on my side. Dirk would not live to see another day. "He killed our Alpha. The rules are clear—we are entitled to a blood tribute of an equivalent kind."

"An equival—"

"The only equivalent is an Alpha," I continued, my voice holding steady. "They killed our Alpha. We demand the Alpha of the Miancarem pack as retribution for their crime."

"That's barbaric!" he spat.

And killing my father in cold blood while his wife, son, and closest friends stood by and watched was civilized?

"It's pack rule," I answered.

I crossed my arms over my chest to keep my hands from shaking. I wanted blood. Dirk Keller's blood.

CHAPTER 8

MY CONVERSATION WITH the council member went almost as I'd anticipated. What I said surprised him, but he didn't dispute that the rules were on my side and my pack was entitled to retribution. Unfortunately, he refused to deliver the tribute until he conferred with the entire council. Apparently ordering a man to his death was beyond the scope of his authority. Or so he claimed. I suspected he was hoping another council member would find a way out of it or, that given more time, I'd calm down and change my mind. He was wrong on both counts.

I had researched every aspect of the rules about tributes, so I knew I had Dirk Keller dead to rights. He killed my father and I would have his blood, even if that meant waiting an extra day so the interpack council could approve my claim and gather my tribute. I could keep my wolf locked down long enough for that. And in the meantime, I tried to think of who would make the best Alpha for our pack once I was gone.

Maybe it was hubris, but no matter how many times I went over the pack member rolls, I couldn't come up with anyone who I would trust to lead my pack. Nobody else had trained for it. Nobody else understood what it meant to lead. Nobody else had studied and prepared.

I was more a brain man than a gut man, always had been. When my father used to ask me what my gut said, I always wondered what he meant.

"How do you feel, Samuel?" he'd say. "Not what do you think up here." He'd tap his head. "What do you feel down here?" He'd pat his belly. "Go with your gut."

All those years and I never understood, but suddenly, I thought maybe I did. Maybe that feeling in my belly telling me to keep trying, telling me there was something I was missing, telling me to look harder, maybe that was my gut. Too bad my father wasn't there to see it.

Bleeding and suffering and then dying. That was the fate Dirk Keller faced for what he did. My mouth salivated, and my muscles tensed in preparation for the destruction I planned to wage on his body.

As if my bloodlust made it so, my phone rang. I expected it to be work related because shifters tended to show up rather than call, but I was wrong.

"This is Samuel Goodwin," I said, using my typical greeting.

"Samuel, this is Anthony Lang. The council discussed your demand for retribution, and while you're technically correct, we were hoping you would reconsid—"

"When will he be brought to me?" I asked. "Or do you want me to gather some men and go to Miancarem to pick him up?" I enjoyed the idea of taking Dirk Keller in front of his pack and humiliating him.

Never in my life had I felt a stronger emotion than the hate that filled me at the thought of the man who took my father. Part of me wondered if it was because my wolf was so close to the surface and so frustrated at being caged. Another part of me wondered if it was because I was broken and unable to feel normal emotions, something I'd heard whispered behind my back for as long as I could remember. Most of me didn't care about the reason.

"We know you're upset and you have every right to be, but two wrongs don't—"

He thought spouting clichés would change my mind? I wanted blood and the delay only fueled my anger.

"Here or there?" I snapped.

Anthony sighed and said, "Don't go on to Miancarem's territory and don't allow your pack to go there, either. The last thing we need is a full-scale battle between neighboring packs. The council will handle this."

"When?"

My voice shook with the strain of keeping my body in check. My wolf wanted out. He wanted to run and claw and bite and kill. No. Not he. We were one and the same, my animal and my human. I wanted those things.

"This is a sensitive situation, and we would appreciate having as much time as possible to deal with it."

I suspected the council would delay the inevitable for as long as they could get away with it. Maybe some of the members were friends with Dirk Keller. Whatever the reason, I didn't know how much time I had left. So even though it was rude to make demands on a council member, I said, "Two weeks have already passed. We need him here by tomorrow."

"Fine," Anthony said resignedly. "We'll deliver your tribute tomorrow."

Knowing I wasn't the only person who lost his Alpha, I notified my pack that we'd succeeded in obtaining vengeance. I offered anybody who wanted a piece of Dirk to come to the Alpha house— my house—and witness his downfall. Only a handful of people took me up on my offer; it seemed the council member wasn't alone in his opinion that a blood tribute was barbaric. But not wanting to see something with their own eyes didn't equate to not wanting it to happen. In fact, based on the expressions on the pack members' faces when they heard the news, I knew I had raised myself in their esteem.

The next morning a dozen shifters, including my father's closest friends, their sons, and Rick Collins, the man who wanted to take my place as Alpha, arrived. We stood together behind the house, each lost in our own thoughts, as we waited for Dirk Keller to be delivered. I would get the first piece of him, there was no question about that, but I could share. Once I finished, the others would have the opportunity to shift and seek their own revenge. If there was anything left of his body when we were done, I'd box it up and send it to his family for burial; I wasn't a complete animal.

My plan was solid, I was certain, so when we heard a vehicle come up the gravel driveway, I felt only anticipation, no dread. I longed to run out front, yank Dirk from the car, and eviscerate him, but I had told Anthony Lang where we'd be, so I remained in place and waited.

The first indication something wasn't right was the silence. Dirk Keller was never silent. Rude, loud, nasty, and confrontational, yes—but not silent. And unless they'd knocked him out or gagged him, I couldn't imagine he'd pick the day he was dragged from his home and his pack and marched to his death to be the day he finally stopped talking.

The reason for what seemed like out-of-character behavior became clear when Anthony Lang and Heath Farbis turned the corner. They were marching a man between them, his arms behind his back, seemingly bound together. But the man wasn't Dirk Keller. It was Korban.

Before my brain could process what I was seeing, my wolf started exploding underneath my skin. I couldn't talk, couldn't see, couldn't move. I burned from the inside out, the pain excruciating. I didn't know how long it lasted, but I was ready to give up, give in, let my wolf have control of my body and go live in the woods alone.

Then out of nowhere, the inner voice that had calmed me after my father's death returned. It felt like a caress inside my head, which should have been a bad thing, because I didn't like being touched, but it wasn't bad; it was comforting. My lungs relaxed, my breathing evened, and I focused on the words coming out of Anthony Lang's mouth.

"Where do you want him?" he asked, his lips pinched and his forehead wrinkled.

"Why is Korban here?" I rasped, hoarse from the exertion taking place underneath my skin.

"You demanded a tribute," Anthony said. "Don't tell me you forgot."

They were trying to replace Dirk with his son? My entire body trembled with rage, probably because I'd been looking forward to killing Dirk and they were delaying my pleasure.

"An equivalent tribute," I barked, stomping over to them. "They killed our Alpha! We are entitled to their Alpha as retribution, not his son." Not Korban.

"He is the Alpha of the Miancarem pack," Heath said tiredly as he pointed at Korban. "You demanded an equivalent tribute and we brought you one, Samuel."

My stomach dropped, and my skin tingled with sweat even though I was suddenly ice-cold. "You can't just name him as Alpha in order to satisfy our demand for retribution. That isn't how the rules work."

"Watch yourself, Samuel." Anthony's voice held a warning note. "We know your father was killed and you're under tremendous stress. We understand the rules are on your side. But do not accuse the council of malicious intent. Dirk Keller was severely wounded during the battle and he hasn't regained consciousness. Even if he does, he is no longer Alpha of the Miancarem pack. The council stripped him of his role the moment we confirmed the contents of the syringe. A man who cheats during a challenge to the death cannot be trusted to lead a pack."

What they said made perfect sense, so much so that I should have figured it out on my own. Not the part about the severity of Dirk's injuries; I had been too enraged during the battle to notice that. But I should have realized the council would strip Dirk of his position.

With my pack members standing behind me and the council members standing in front of me, I desperately tried to undo what I had done. Killing Korban Keller had never been my plan.

"What does it matter?" someone said. It took me several moments to realize it was Rick Collins. "We are owed a blood tribute and we received one."

He probably thought he was impressing the men around us with that comment, probably assumed it would help him displace me as Alpha. I hoped he was wrong. My father wouldn't have supported that type of behavior. For a moment, I wondered if my father would have supported what I'd been seeking—retribution from the man who killed him. But then Rick stole my attention.

He sneered, walked toward Korban, and said, "Let's get on with it."

"Step back." I growled at him, the sound unlike any I'd heard; it wasn't human. I bared my teeth as I jumped between him and Korban. "He's mine!"

The words were out of my mouth before they went through my brain. Rick stumbled back, looking pale, and the rest of my pack members flinched. I'd terrified my own pack. Truth be told, I'd scared myself with the intensity of my reaction. Admittedly, my plan had been to take the first shot at our tribute, but I didn't need to make my own pack members feel threatened to accomplish that. I tried to breathe and curb the desire to rip out Rick's throat. What was wrong with me?

"You're an honorable man," Heath whispered hoarsely.

He was behind me, so I turned at the sound of his voice. He was talking to Korban, leaning toward him. Every hair on my body stood on end.

"We realize it wasn't easy to walk away from your pack and come here, but you did it without a fight, and for that we thank you." Heath closed his eyes and swallowed hard. "I wish it could be different, Korban," he said, his voice breaking.

He reached for Korban, and my skin prickled as my wolf raged forward. I didn't blink, didn't so much as breathe, hoping I could keep that part of myself back. It wasn't the time to lose control. Not there, not in front of everyone, not when I wouldn't be able to find my way back.

Navy blue eyes met my gaze, and Korban moved away from Heath. "Don't be sorry," Korban said, speaking for the first time that day. "This is where I'm supposed to be."

I hadn't heard his voice in five years, and the sound of it shot through me like a bolt of lightning. Before I knew what I was doing, I was beside Korban, my hand clamped around his arm, my chest rumbling with a roar that threatened to escape.

"The council will not sanction you for any action taken against your tribute," Heath said, his gaze cold as it landed on me. "But we won't stay to witness it."

Something was wrong. I had been looking forward to this, craving my opportunity to make Dirk Keller pay. It turned out he'd paid in more ways than I'd anticipated—he was deeply injured, possibly dying; he'd lost his pack, and now he'd lost his son. I should have been happy, but instead, my mind was in a haze, my body ached, and my stomach rolled. This wasn't right.

Don't worry, the calming voice whispered in my head. Everything will be okay.

I heard the council members walk to the front of the house, heard their vehicle start, heard the crunch of gravel as they drove away, and through it all, I didn't move. I couldn't move.

"Let's get on with it," Rick said once again, only this time his voice was hesitant, his posture hunched and nonthreatening.

It seemed I had intimidated him, which pleased me. I was less pleased to see the wary gazes directed my way from my father's closest friends. People had looked at him with respect and admiration. I wasn't supposed to lead through fear; I would have known that even if he hadn't told me. And he had told me. Many times.

We used to sit around the kitchen table late into the night talking about the pack, talking about what they needed. He explained connections, trust, loyalty. He taught me about leading with a firm but always gentle hand. He shared all the wisdom he had gained from his years as Alpha, from his own father, and from his grandfather.

As a child, I thought my father knew all the answers to all the questions in the universe. In more recent years, I thought he expected the unattainable and didn't always make sense. On that day, with important men from my pack around me and Korban Keller beside me, all I could think was that I wasn't ready to be Alpha. I wanted my father back.

Shhh, the voice in my head said. You're ready. You can do this. It's going to be fine.

Those words sounded familiar. Were they something my father had said?

George Griffin, my father's friend, cleared his throat to get my attention. "Samuel, if you're not ready to do this—"

"I can do it," Rick said, puffing his chest but not getting any closer to me. "I'm strong enough to do it."

It wasn't a matter of strength. Without releasing my grasp on Korban, I looked him over. He was taller than my own five feet eleven inches, but only by an inch or two. Our builds were similar: both muscular but in a lanky way, not bulky. His hair was still golden, his skin fair and freckled, both of which made him look the part of an innocent angel rather than a strong Alpha. His blue eyes, though... They were all steely strength. Nobody could underestimate him if they were looking in his eyes.

But strength wasn't enough for a man whose hands were bound behind his back and who faced not only one shifter, but a dozen. Korban wouldn't leave our land alive and he had to know that, and yet he looked peaceful, unafraid. He didn't argue, didn't fight, didn't beg. He simply stood and stared at me, patiently waiting for something, and I found myself desperately trying to figure out what it was. Once again, Korban Keller had me unbalanced. It was just like when we were kids.

"Quit stalling, Alpha," Rick said, managing to turn what should have been an honorific into a barb.

A couple of the younger men, who I knew were his friends, snickered. They were sons of some of my father's friends, and I wondered what they thought. I wondered what my father would have thought.

"I told you he was off," Rick whispered.

I had great hearing, so I had no problem making out his words, which I was about to point out when Bradley Griffin, one of his friends, answered, his voice even lower but still audible enough for my ears to pick up. "I think he's scared."

"How can he lead us if he's too scared to take on a guy who's all tied up?" said Damon Huntsworth, the third man my age.

I was confused by Korban's lack of reaction and frustrated by the insults from the men my age. But what put me over the edge were the expressions on the faces of my father's friends. My father had looked at me the same way when I couldn't understand his lessons: sad, disappointed, and worried.

"Let's end this," I barked, not sure if I was referring to their doubts, to my confusion, or to Korban's life. Maybe it was all three.

My father would have reminded me about empathy and compassion. He would have said I had to be flexible and adjust to what was going on around me. But I wasn't my father and I didn't know how to do those things.

So instead, I jerked the arm I was holding, and Korban followed me without a word. When we reached the center of the yard, I put my hand on his shoulder and shoved him down. Once again, he complied easily, lowering himself to his knees without protest.

Until that point, my body had been fighting with my brain. My instincts had been telling me something was wrong, that I had to stop. My brain had been saying I had to exact vengeance, had to gain the respect of my pack. And then in that confusing moment, with my father's friends behind me, looking hopeful, and the men my age beside me, waiting to see if I could prove my strength, Korban bowed his head, revealing his long, smooth neck.

Without further pause or thought, I snapped and lunged forward, burying my canines in his skin. It wasn't the way I had planned it. I had intended to demolish my tribute while in my wolf form, using my claws and teeth and animal strength. Blood and screams wouldn't hound my wolf; that part of me would appreciate the hunt. As I licked hot skin and swallowed Korban's life essence, my head cleared and realizations came into focus.

I hadn't bitten his jugular, but had instead landed with my teeth in the spot where his neck met his shoulder.

He hadn't screamed.

We were both in our human forms.

And I was aroused, so very aroused. My veins strummed and my cock throbbed. That was wrong. No matter how good and right it felt, it had to be wrong. I had to stop, had to pull away from him, had to gain control of myself. But before I could, pure pleasure flowed from my mouth to my chest to my groin, and I spilled myself in my pants.

As soon as I realized what had happened, I leaped up. Korban slumped forward and collapsed onto the grass, his body curled into a ball, his hands still bound behind his back. For one horrible, terrifying moment, I thought I killed him.

Why I was relieved when I noticed movement in his back and realized he was breathing, I couldn't say. He was a blood tribute. I was supposed to kill him.

What I wasn't supposed to do was pierce his skin with my mouth in my human form.

What I wasn't supposed to do was enjoy his flavor on my tongue.

What I wasn't supposed to do was come in my pants from the pleasure those things brought me.

I was a monster; a true monster. "Put him in the workshop," I rasped, pointing to a building behind the house where my father kept his tools and lumber. "Nobody else touch him."

Before anybody could argue, I turned on my heel and ran into the forest. I couldn't control my temper, couldn't control my body, couldn't control my thoughts, but I could still enjoy the scents and sounds of nature. I could still run.

CHAPTER 9

I FLED THE scene I'd created in my own backyard and managed to reach the trees before shifting into my wolf. Before I'd been forced to lock my wolf down, shifting into my animal form had been my favorite way to relax. I loved feeling the wind in my fur and the soil under my paws. I loved the respite from doubts and pressures. And I loved the freedom to run.

With my wolf finally in control, my logical mind whispered that I'd never return. In that form I always ran away from our pack lands, even back when I had a family to come home to. Without my father, mother, and siblings waiting for me in Yafenack, I had no reason to go back.

Except this time, I didn't run away, or at least I didn't run far. I was still within our pack lands when I veered left instead of continuing straight. That path took me in a circle, not returning home, but not straying far from it, either. Around I went, racing against the confusing feelings within myself but unable to escape them.

Instead of easing my tension, the shift seemed to exacerbate it. My wolf was restless, needy, panicked. Something was missing, and because I didn't know what it was, I couldn't figure out how to fix it. The only thing I could do was run faster and harder and hope I could escape myself.

But then I heard a yelp. I skidded to a halt, lifted my chin, and perked my ears up. The sound came again, raising my hairs on end. That was Korban Keller. I didn't know how I knew, but I did.

Without conscious thought, I hustled toward the source of the sound. It didn't take long before another of my senses picked up Korban—I could smell his blood. Howling to the sky, I sped up my pace.

I had bitten him, but not enough to make his blood flow. When I'd left him, he had been on the ground, but not wounded, not bleeding. What had they done to him?

The scene I'd left had been confusing; the one that greeted me when I returned was utter chaos. The noises and scents were coming from the workshop, so I went straight there. The older pack members—my father's friends—were gone. Korban was crouched in a corner in human form, clutching a shovel. The bindings were gone from his wrists, but his skin was raw in the spots where they'd been. His torso was covered in scratches and bites, and there was rope hanging off one of his ankles, so I guessed they'd bound his legs after I left.

Rick Collins, Damon Huntsworth, and Paul Strickland were in their wolf forms. They'd formed a semicircle around Korban, baring their teeth and jumping forward, trying to get to him while avoiding the shovel he swung.

I growled and clawed at the nearest body, gouging Paul's skin and making him yip in pain. All three wolves turned to look at me. It was a remarkably stupid move, because it left their backs to the man they'd been attacking and who was brandishing a weapon.

Surprisingly, Korban didn't take advantage of the opportunity. He remained in place, white-knuckling the shovel and watching. He was always watching.

Though I wanted to shift into my human form to ask my pack members why they hadn't listened to my order and to punish them for daring to attack my tribute, I couldn't. My wolf was enraged, full of emotion and power and want. I had no idea how to sate my beast and I stood no chance of releasing myself from that form while I was in that condition.

So instead, I slowly stalked my pack members, my chest rumbling, my lips curled over my teeth. My anger felt like a living, breathing thing, and I wasn't sure I could control it, wasn't sure I wanted to. I'd had enough of Rick questioning me, enough of them whispering about me, enough of people doubting me. I'd had enough.

My roar shook the walls of the wooden building with its volume and intensity. I'd never made a sound like that, never heard a sound like that. Immediately, Damon and Paul rolled onto their backs and showed me their bellies before shifting into their human forms and cowering. I enjoyed seeing their submission, but it wasn't enough to sate me.

Rick remained in his wolf form, his gaze darting between mine and the ground, like he was trying to stand tall, trying to best me, but wasn't completely sure he could. I, on the other hand, was sure I was the stronger shifter, so I pounced, landing on top of him with my jaws around his throat.

Though I didn't like him, he was my pack member, and my father said an Alpha cared for his pack, taught his pack. So I gave him a chance to submit, shaking his neck without snapping it. But when he kept growling and moving, fighting my control, my dominance, I lost my patience. I didn't care about Rick, didn't know what I could teach him, wasn't sure why it mattered anyway. He would stop challenging me, either on his own or because I ended his life. Both options held appeal.

I'd tightened my bite, pressing my canines against his skin, almost digging in, when I heard the voice in my head.

Balance your strength with compassion, Samuel. He failed in his mission to impress the pack. Be patient; wait for him to relent.

Patience, compassion. Those were things my father discussed often. The realization stopped me from piercing Rick's skin, but I still trembled with adrenaline and rage.

Shhh, the voice whispered. Wait. Just wait.

My muscles relaxed, the pressure in my chest loosened, and my breathing evened. I still held Rick immobile, still showed him my dominance, but I was no longer on the edge of losing control.

That's right. Just like that.

Within a few seconds, the furry body below me whimpered and then shifted into his human form. I remained in place and stared into his eyes until he darted his gaze away.

"You said we could have him once you were done," Rick said hoarsely. "Then you left, so we thought we could. We thought he was ours—"

I tightened my jaw and growled low in my throat to show my displeasure at his lie. I had told them to put Korban in the workshop. I hadn't given them permission to attack him. He was mine. I jolted at the thought.

No. He wasn't mine. He was a tribute. The pack lost an Alpha. The tribute was for the pack. The logic didn't change the feeling in my gut.

"I told you we shouldn't have come back. Our dads tied him up. That's how we should have left him," Damon said.

"But he's a tribute!" Rick answered.

I clamped down harder.

"I'm sorry," he whispered, his voice strained.

Realizing I was holding him too tight for him to talk and probably too tight for him to breathe, I backed off. He scrambled away, clutching his neck and looking at me warily.

I barked and stepped forward.

"Alpha!" he yelled, and he tilted his head, showing me his neck, which was already red and was sure to show bruises by the end of the day. "I'm sorry, Alpha."

Stopping my advance, I glared at the men, bared my teeth, and gave a low, rumbling growl, telling them to leave. Without further argument, they backed out of the workshop. I listened to their footsteps as they ran away and remained on guard until I knew they were gone. As out of sorts as I was, it took me some time to ask myself what I was guarding and who I was guarding it from.

Rick wasn't a nice man, but he was a member of my pack. His friends I didn't know well, but they were also part of my pack. I was responsible for them. And yet I'd attacked them, scared them, pushed them away.

My father wouldn't have done any of those things. He would have found a way to calm the situation without frightening his pack. One of the lessons he'd taught me was that an Alpha didn't lower himself to those around him; instead he raised others up. And yet at the first opportunity, I plummeted down to Rick's level. When I asked myself why, I realized I already knew the answer.

It was him. Korban Keller. He was the reason I came back to my house instead of fleeing to the safety of the deep woods. He was the reason I'd gone against my pack. It was like being eight years old all over again, only this time Korban had managed to confuse and manipulate me from a distance. Fear wasn't the same as respect, my father used to say, and now my pack members feared me. It was Korban's fault.

Slowly, I turned around and narrowed my eyes at the man who had worked to make me feel out of sorts for as long as I'd known him, the man whose father killed my father, the man who had forced me to behave in a way that would divide me from my pack.

The adrenaline thrumming through my body fueled my rage. He had been able to ward off three of my pack members with that shovel, but I would show Korban Keller I was the stronger wolf. Raising my head, I howled long and loud, reminding my animal how it felt to be free and proud and strong. Then I lunged.

I expected Korban to swing his weapon at me, like he had been doing with my pack members, but instead, he dropped it, once again confusing me. I jumped on my enemy and found a pure white wolf under me instead of a man. I wondered why he had changed forms instead of keeping his human hands and using the shovel to beat me. Before I could ponder the question for long, Korban's scent invaded my senses, along with the heat of his body. My goal had been to kill him, but once again, I clamped my mouth over the intersection of his neck and shoulder, rather than his jugular.

Everything after that moment was a blur. My mind went white, then dark, and then pulsed with fire. I heard growling and whining. I smelled and tasted blood. I felt strength pushing back against my own. Pure, undiluted pleasure consumed me. And then there was nothing.

Panting woke me. Or maybe that wasn't the right description. I couldn't have been asleep; it was more like my brain had checked out of my body. But the sound of heavy breathing slammed it back into my head. I was still in my wolf form, which wasn't a surprise. I doubted I'd ever be able to shift back.

I blinked my eyes open and saw fur. White fur. It was under me and it smelled amazing. So amazing, in fact, that my belly tightened and my groin pulsed, bringing my attention to that part of my body.

Never in my entire life had I felt anything like it. The warmth, the silky softness, the tight pressure; my dick was encased in slick heat. I moved experimentally and realized I couldn't go far. Confused, I tried again, and then it hit me—I was tied; that was why I couldn't move away. The mating knot at the base of my cock kept me in place, kept me connected to someone.

After that revelation, my mind moved quickly and sharply. I knew the scent surrounding me, knew the wolf beneath me. It was Korban Keller. I had attacked him, overpowered him, penetrated him, and tied with him.

Whining in horror at what I'd done, I wiggled and sighed in relief when my body finally allowed me to pop free. With a whimper, Korban raised his head and twisted it back to look at me. Immediately, I turned away. Those blue eyes in his wolf body would be no less powerful than they were in his human one.

However Korban had treated me, however much he had confused me and made me feel on guard and off-balance, he didn't deserve what I'd done to him. Nobody did. Not trusting myself in his presence, I backed out of the workshop. I needed to bind him with the rope so he wouldn't escape, but I couldn't get that close to Korban after the way I'd just treated him.

Instinctively, I shifted into my human form and slammed the door shut. It wasn't until I had my hand wrapped around the cool metal padlock that I realized I'd shifted and it wasn't difficult. I couldn't remember the last time I'd done that with ease.

The recovery from the shameful problem I'd kept hidden from all but my immediate family seemed like a miracle until I realized I'd tied. I couldn't understand why I'd done it. Losing control of my wolf after I'd kept that part of myself caged made sense. Our animals needed to feel the air just as much as our humans and denying ourselves that didn't come easily or naturally, so whenever my animal form took over, I ran without thought.

But there was nothing natural about losing control of myself to do what I'd just done to Korban. And there was nothing natural about the feelings pulsing inside me at that moment. I wanted to go back into the workshop. I wanted to look into the blue eyes that had searched for me. I wanted to inhale the sweet scent that had surrounded me. I wanted to feel Korban's warmth against my body.

My fingers trembled as I clicked the padlock closed. Hoping it would hold him until I gained control of myself, I dashed toward the house and away from the sick temptation. Until I'd misled them, my father and mother had thought my lack of tying was the source of my shifting issue, and though I had been too ashamed to tell them the truth, I had spent years trying unsuccessfully to find a female who could inspire that part of me. I didn't understand why I had done with a male that which I hadn't been able to convince my body to do with females in packs both near and far.

And I didn't understand why I wanted to do it again. No. Not wanted. Needed.

Cringing in horror at myself, I ran into the house and locked the back door. I stumbled through the family room, bile rising as I thought of what I'd done to Korban. That feeling mixed with a spike of need as I ran my hand across my mouth and realized I smelled different; I smelled like him. My palms tingled with the desire to connect with his skin.

"No!" I screamed to myself. "No!"

I had to get his scent off my body. Surely that would solve one of my problems. Racing through the house, I knocked over a lamp, bumped into the edge of a sofa table, and stubbed my toe on the bottom of the stairs. My wolf started scratching at me, wanting to get out, wanting to go back outside, back to Korban.

What was wrong with me?

"No!" I yelled again, thumping into the hallway walls. "Please, no."

I managed to make it to the bathroom and dropped to my knees in front of the toilet just as my stomach emptied its contents. I had to control myself. I had to stop myself.

Crawling into the shower, I shivered and ignored the wetness streaking down my cheeks. I reached for the handle, turned it so the water would be as hot as I could bear, and sat under the spray, hoping it could wash away my sins—both the one I'd committed just outside the house, and the ones I longed to commit again.

Dropping my head on my knees, I let the tears flow. "No."

CHAPTER 10

I COULDN'T SLEEP. My mind was a jumble of recollections—flashes of Korban from over the years—all mingled together. My memory wasn't bad, but it wasn't great either, and the things I tended to remember were facts or goals. This was different.

I remembered Korban's expressions when he had looked at me, the twinkle in his eyes and the warmth of his smile, which didn't make sense because I knew without a doubt that at the time I had told myself both were sinister. I remembered things he had said that should have been meaningless and forgotten the next day, but had wedged themselves into my brain. I remembered running with him in our wolf forms and feeling free and whole, which was strange because at the time I had tried to banish the experience from my mind. I remembered having my first orgasm right in front of him, which was something I'd never done fully clothed without a touch to my genitals since that day. I remembered laughing with him, which was odd because I wasn't the laughing type.

But most of all, I remembered how I had felt when I was with Korban. There was confusion and discomfort, but overall there was a deep sense of peace and safety. With that realization in place, I had to ask myself why I hated him.

For as long as I could remember, I had told myself to stay away from Korban, told myself something wasn't right with him, something wasn't safe. The only answer I could come up with was that deep inside I had always known that something was wrong with me and that being with him brought it to the surface.

I had to stay away from him. It was the only solution. And I tried. I tried really hard. But I was exhausted; I couldn't remember the last time I had slept for more than a couple of hours, and the need to see Korban again, to smell Korban again, to touch Korban again, was insistent, unrelenting, and bone-deep. So after about a day, I broke. My excuse was that he hadn't eaten.

The council members had delivered him to us the previous morning, and the sun had already set. The workshop had a toilet and a sink. I hadn't bound his hands, so he had access to water. And though he could survive longer without food, with the energy he had exerted shifting, he was sure to be hungry. Very hungry.

Pacing back and forth across my kitchen, I tried to decide if I could trust myself to bring him something to eat and quickly leave. I had already dismissed the idea of killing him, knowing I wouldn't be able to do it myself and wouldn't tolerate anybody else doing it. Korban wasn't the one who killed my father, and I wouldn't allow his life to be taken in retribution for an act that wasn't his own. I had blamed him far too many times for my own shortcomings.

Unfortunately, I had demanded the Miancarem Alpha as a tribute, loudly and repeatedly, and then bragged about it to my pack. Setting him free would surely be seen as a sign of tremendous weakness, which would reflect badly on my entire pack. So I wouldn't kill him, but I couldn't set him free.

I didn't know what to do. I couldn't think straight. And I had a prisoner—a prisoner—in my yard.

With a growl of frustration, I dragged my fingers through my hair, stomped over to the refrigerator, and yanked out sandwich fixings. I slammed everything onto the counter and started what was surely the angriest sandwich preparation of all time. A few minutes later, I stuffed a couple of sandwiches, an apple, an orange, and a bag of chips into a plastic bag, grabbed the key out of the bowl, and walked outside.

My anger turned to caution as I neared the workshop. Strangely, I wasn't worried about Korban attacking me, even though I was alone and he wasn't bound. Instead, I was concerned about the clawing need inside myself. I knew that feeling well—it was my body wanting to shift, my wolf wanting to come out. Logic took a backseat to instincts in that form, and my instincts were wrong. No way could I trust myself around Korban that way.

Stopping in my tracks, I closed my eyes and took a deep breath. I had to calm down and stay that way. I had to keep myself under control.

When I thought I was ready, I finished the short walk to the workshop, moving slowly so I could focus on breathing, on keeping my mind clear, on staying in my human form. I slipped the bag handles over my wrist and raised the key to the lock. With another deep breath, I felt settled and ready. I unlocked the padlock, opened the door, walked inside, and lost my hold on all that hard-fought sanity.

He was naked, which, if I had thought it through, I should have expected. He had shifted under me when I'd... He had shifted under me. That meant his clothes had been destroyed.

His back was to me, his legs spread, and he was bent over, standing in front of the sink and using fabric—possibly a piece of his shirt—to scrub his legs. Everything I saw came at me in fast, sharp flashes.

His pale, smooth skin.

His lean, corded muscles.

His strong, furry thighs.

His round, full ass.

His wrinkled sac.

His flaccid dick.

I gasped, which drew his attention.

He straightened and turned around. "Samuel," he said as he looked at me. "I'm glad you're here. I want to—"

Everything happened too quickly, or maybe I was thinking too slowly, but whatever the reason, I didn't manage to avoid his gaze, and when his blue eyes locked with mine, my control snapped. I heard the bag I held fall to the floor. I heard the door slam behind me when I lost my grip on it. I heard a cry and realized it was me. I felt my perspective change as fur covered my body and I landed on four legs.

Somewhere along the way, Korban's eyes widened and then he shifted. His reaction was probably instinct, his wolf preparing to defend himself from a shifter bracing for a fight. He should have been able to defend himself from me; he was bigger, stronger, and saner. Maybe he was weak from hunger, or maybe he thought I had reinforcements outside the door, or maybe he was taken off guard by the type of assault I waged. Whatever the reason, within minutes, I found myself in the same position I'd been in the previous day—in my wolf form, tied to Korban Keller, with my teeth buried in his skin.

I wanted to release him from the pain I was sure I was causing, but I couldn't. With my mating knot swollen inside him, I had effectively trapped him. Raising my head, I howled in sorrow.

I hated what I'd done to him, hated that I hadn't been able to stop myself from doing it again, hated myself. As soon as I was able, I scrambled away until I bumped against the door. After shifting into my human form, once again with no trouble, I scrambled for my clothes. They weren't wearable.

"Samuel," Korban said, getting my attention.

I snapped my head up. "I'm sorry." Clutching my clothes to my chest, I backed out of the workshop. "I'm so sorry."

"Wait!"

He thought he could talk to me, thought some sort of logic would save him from his fate, but he was wrong. My brain had stopped functioning, and my body had traded one ailment—the inability to control my shift—for a much worse condition. If I stayed in that room with Korban, I'd hurt him again, I was certain of it.

I slammed the door and heard a jingling sound. My keys. I reached down, grabbed them, fumbled with the lock, and then ran back to my house, intent on getting away from Korban as fast as possible.

The night before I had been focused on myself, on what was wrong with me. I'd wasted time in the shower, wasted time thinking, wasted time pacing. No more.

My father used to tell me a man's character could be measured by what he did when he thought nobody was looking. When nobody was looking, I turned into a monster. I couldn't stop hurting Korban and give him his life back, so I'd end my own.

Knowing I owed it to my pack to find someone to care for them and that I needed to ensure that whoever that was would set Korban free, I forced myself to stop being selfish, stop thinking about my failings, and start thinking about who I could contact for help. Within minutes, I thought of a name: Zev Hassick.

He was the Alpha of the Etzgadol pack, and though he was one of the younger Alphas, in less than a decade, he'd grown his pack to be the largest in North America. My father had always spoken highly of him and said Zev shared his philosophies about leadership and how to treat nonshifters. And my mother's close friends lived in his pack, which was why she had taken my siblings and run there when she needed to escape the tragedy that had befallen our home.

Yes. Zev Hassick was a good choice. He would know what to do about my pack. He would take care of Korban.

My need for organization and keeping up with modern times meant I had a spreadsheet with contact information for every pack and every Alpha. I took the stairs three at a time, raced to my room, and found Zev's number.

"Hello," a deep, rumbling voice answered after a couple of rings.

"Zev Hassick?"

"Yes."

"This is Samuel Goodwin. We've never met, but you know... knew my father, Tom Goodwin. He is...was Alpha of the—"

"Your father was a good man," Zev said. "I'm very sorry for your loss and the circumstances surrounding it." He paused. "How are you holding up, Samuel?"

For years, I had lied when my father had asked if I was okay. I had minimized my shifting problem and intentionally misled him about my tying problem. Not anymore. I would no longer hide my weakness because of my pride.

"Not good," I answered honestly. Licking my lips, I took a deep breath. "I need your help, Alpha. For my pack."

"I'll help in any way I can. Tell me what you need."

Drawing in another deep breath, I tried to think clearly enough to choose the right words. "I've been raised to take over as Alpha since I was born. There's nobody else with the training, and if... something happens to me, I'm worried harm will come to my pack."

"What's going to happen to you?" Zev asked, his voice changing timbre in a way that made me tense. My father had described him as a kind leader, but his tone screamed danger. "Has Dirk Keller healed? Is he a threat again?"

I was surprised Zev knew about Dirk, but then I realized what he had done, both the challenge and killing my father, were so out of the ordinary that any Alpha with connections to the interpack council was sure to have heard of it. Zev was powerful enough that his name had been whispered as a replacement the next time there was an opening on the council, which was rare for a man in his thirties.

"No, he hasn't healed. At least I don't think so."

"Good." Zev sighed in relief. "And how is Korban holding up?"

Yet another surprise. Why would Zev know Korban Keller? And why would he think I'd have any information about him? The only possible reason was if he knew I'd demanded the Miancarem Alpha as a tribute, but then he would surely think Korban was dead.

"You know Korban?" I said, trying to put the thoughts swimming in my head into some sort of logical order.

"Yes. My mate has family in Miancarem, and he likes to visit them from time to time. I've never thought much of Dirk Keller, but Jonah and I have always respected Korban, so we spend time with him when we're there." He sighed. "That apple fell in a different hemisphere from the tree."

He likes to visit his family. Jonah.

"You're mated to a male?"

There was a pause before Zev answered, sounding confused. "Yes. He's my true mate."

"True mate?" I said disbelievingly.

True mates were exceedingly rare. Most shifters met another shifter and chose to take them as their mate. They tied together time and again, allowing the male to keep hold of his humanity and releasing the female's wolf.

But if a shifter had a true mate, no other would do. True mates were connected completely—soul to heart, skin to bones. They could hold on to both halves only by tying with each other because they were in fact one, two halves of a whole needing to connect their bodies and their lives to be complete. Though I'd never met a pair of true mates, I'd read about them in the writings. Having a true mate was considered a blessing, the best gift a shifter could receive.

To hear a male had taken another male as a mate turned everything I'd learned about tying on its head. To hear a male had another male for a true mate contradicted the very essence of what I'd read about our people and how we were made.

"How?" I rasped, my voice rough with confusion, disbelief, and a nagging thought I couldn't quite catch.

"I thought you knew. Didn't he tell you?"

I didn't realize my father spoke with Zev outside of meetings, and given how infrequently those happened and how busy they were focusing on pack business, it wasn't likely he would have known anything about Zev's mate based on conversations during the meetings.

"No." I shook my head even though he couldn't see me. My head pounded and my heart raced. I felt like I was missing something important, but I didn't know what it was. What I did know was that a male couldn't mate with another male. It wasn't possible. "Males have to tie with females in order to hold on to their human halves. That's—"

"Bullshit."

I was going to say it was basic biology. "What do you mean?"

"Tying isn't about males and females. It's about connecting with someone who can better you, someone who can give you what you're lacking, someone who can fulfill you and make you whole." Zev sighed. "We tie with our mates on all levels—physical and emotional—so we can become the best versions of ourselves. That's what makes us complete, and then we're stable enough to bind both our forms—wolf and human."

"That isn't in the writings," I mumbled, more to myself than to him.

"The writings are old and incomplete. They were written by shifters who had a very narrow view of our people and a dangerously bigoted view of nonshifters," he said in disgust. "It's our job as Alphas to help our packs grow past those mistakes, to teach them that shifters can be stronger by living in the world instead of apart from it, and that we can follow our instincts instead of being limited by rules created by those who are long gone."

The way he spoke, with conviction, passion, and not a small dose of frustration, led me to believe it wasn't the first time Zev Hassick had given that speech. It was a lot of information to process in a short period of time and it left me reeling. So much so that I forgot the reason for my call. Apparently, I also forgot to speak.

"Didn't Korban explain this to you?" Zev asked when I'd stayed silent for too long.

I suddenly understood that when Zev asked whether he had told me, he'd been referring to Korban rather than my father. In some ways, it made more sense. The interactions Zev and my father had were at interpack council meetings, where mates weren't present and were unlikely to be discussed. Plus, if for some reason my father had learned the information, he surely would have shared it with me. But what didn't make sense was why Zev would think a man I was planning to kill would tell me anything.

"Why would Korban—"

A pained cry rent the air and stopped me midsentence. It was closely followed by two more screams. I didn't know who was making the noises or why, but they were coming from behind my house. Where Korban was locked up. Had something happened to Korban?

I dropped the phone and ran out of the room, down the stairs, and out the back door. Shouts were coming from the workshop. With my heart slamming against my rib cage, I flew in that direction.

The door was open. Why was the door open? Had I forgotten to lock it? I got my answer when I saw the padlock lying on the ground. It had been cut off, which terrified me, but not as much as the silence. Screams were bad, but sudden silence afterward was worse. Within seconds, I skidded into the workshop, prepared to defend Korban.

How strange was that? I was going to defend the man I was supposed to kill. The man I held captive. The man I kept assaulting. Defend him from who? I was Korban's biggest threat.

The first thing I registered when I entered the workshop was blood. Korban was covered in it. With a wail, I lunged toward him, forgetting that my presence was sure to cause him fear rather than comfort.

"Samuel," he said, sounding relieved. Lord knew why.

"Where are you hurt?" I ghosted my hands over his skin, not sure where I could touch without damaging him more.

"I'm fine." He glanced down at his body and then back at me. "The blood isn't mine." He flicked his chin to the side. "It's theirs."

I followed his gaze and saw Rick Collins and Jason Clemson slumped against the wall. Based on the way they were holding their faces and the blood streaming down their chins, I gathered their noses were broken.

"What are you doing here?" I growled at my pack members as I stepped toward them. "I made it clear you were supposed to leave."

"We wanted to see if you finally killed the tribute or if you were too weak," Rick said. He might have been going for tough, but with his nose full of blood, he sounded like a goose. Plus, he was trying to stand while he spoke, and he couldn't get his feet under him, so he kept slipping around on nothing. "We saw you leaving earlier." He braced his hand against the wall and finally rose to his feet. "We know what you did to him," he sneered.

My stomach dropped and then rolled. I didn't know what to say.

"It wasn't my idea, Alpha," Jason said. "I didn't know where we were going when he brought me here."

"Leave," I said hoarsely. "Leave now."

I didn't know what Rick saw in my face, but amazingly, he didn't argue or try to show me up. Keeping my attention on him, I watched as he stumbled out of the workshop, holding his arm over his stomach and limping on his right leg. Jason was close behind him, and based on his gait, he wasn't doing any better. When their footsteps faded away entirely, I sighed.

"It's not safe for you out here," I whispered without looking at Korban. I had put him in an untenable position and I had no way to fix it.

"So far mine isn't the safety that's been compromised."

Glancing up at him, I furrowed my brow in confusion. "Huh?"

"My knuckles hurt a little." He grinned, rubbed his palms over the backs of his hands, and tilted his head toward the door. "But unless I'm wrong, those guys have worse problems."

If the scuffle I'd interrupted had been the only issue, he would have been right. But I knew for a fact how badly he had been compromised. After all, I was the one who had done it to him. I didn't know how he could be so lighthearted about everything.

"I know what you're thinking, and you're wrong," he said, his voice lower. He inched toward me.

He couldn't possibly know what I was thinking.

"There were two of them and one of me, and you saw who won."

That was true. Of course, Korban was an Alpha. It was no surprise he was stronger than other shifters.

"And yesterday there were three of them." He took another step. "I didn't let them get what they wanted then, either." He was a hair's distance from me, and he scrunched his eyebrows together in concern. "You look tired, Samuel." He slowly raised his hand and gently placed it on my back, as if I was the one afraid of touch. Well, I supposed I always had been sensitive about my personal space, but his touch was different. His touch had always been different. "When was the last time you got a good night's sleep?"

I shrugged, both because I didn't know the answer to his question and because I couldn't breathe with him so close to me. I didn't want to hurt him again, but I had no idea if I could keep myself from doing it.

"You need to go to bed," he said.

"You're not safe here," I repeated.

"Then I'll come inside with you." He kept his hand on my back and started walking toward the open doorway.

"I can't..." I shook my head and gulped. "You shouldn't be with me. I'm dangerous."

He didn't slow down; he just kept walking, leading us out of the workshop and toward the house.

"No, you're not."

"How can you say that after..." I closed my eyes in shame. "How can you say that?"

"You're a strong shifter, Samuel. Definitely stronger than those two pack members of yours." We reached the back door and Korban opened it. He waited for me to walk inside, and then he followed me, closed the door, and locked it. "But at the risk of ruffling up that pride I remember from when we were kids, I have to ask: Do you actually think you're stronger than me?"

CHAPTER 11

SOME QUESTIONS sounded simple, but they were hard to answer. I had always prided myself on my strength, knowing it would be valuable for my role as Alpha of my pack. And I was quick to get defensive if I felt that strength was questioned, including by Korban. But with him standing naked in front of me, firm muscles on display, power rolling off him, I couldn't deny his strength. I even admired it. Was I stronger than him? Did I want to be?

"You look like you're about to fall over," he said. He sounded concerned, not like he was mocking or judging me, so I didn't argue. "You haven't slept in days, have you?"

I shook my head and focused on keeping myself upright.

"Well, that explains why all that tightly held control finally snapped."

Wincing at the reminder of what I'd done to him when I lost my control, I lowered my gaze and started stepping away so I wouldn't crowd him.

"No." He grasped my shoulder and then eased his hand onto my back. "That wasn't a complaint." He sighed. "We need to talk, but first we need to get you operating on all cylinders, which means sleep. Where's your room?"

Pride should have kept me from letting him decide what I needed and when. Instinct should have prevented me from leading him to the place where I slept and was most vulnerable. Self-respect should have stopped me from giving in to my exhaustion by slumping my shoulders and shuffling my feet as I neared the bedroom. And yet I did all of those things without a second thought or a hint of hesitation.

When we got to the bed, he dropped his hand from my back and waited for me to get in. I shivered, suddenly cold in my core. I looked at him, not sure what I wanted, but certain he could provide it.

"I'm filthy," he said, gesturing to his blood- and dirt-covered body. "You lie down and I'll go wash up."

He was right. I could only imagine how he felt, coated in filth and grime. "I'm sorry. I should have thought to... I shouldn't have put you... I—"

"Shhh." He cupped the back of my head and massaged my scalp. "You need sleep. You can't complete a thought or think straight." He tilted his chin toward the door at the end of my room. "That's the bathroom, right?"

I nodded.

"Take your clothes off and get in bed. I'll be right back."

It wasn't until my shoes and pants were pooled around my ankles and I was stripping my shirt off that I realized what I was doing. Why on earth was I listening to what he said? Why was I putting myself in an exposed and vulnerable position? Why was I letting him bathe in my shower when I normally couldn't stand anyone in my personal space?

"You know why, Samuel."

I darted my gaze up and saw Korban standing in the bathroom doorway, looking at me.

"Did I say that out loud?" I asked.

"No." He shook his head.

"Then how did you—"

He smiled at me, his expression soft. "Sleep, Samuel. You know all of this in here." He tapped his hand against his chest. "You just need to let go of the things you've learned in here"—he tapped the side of his head—"to realize it."

Whether I would have argued or demanded more answers, I'd never know because Korban walked into the bathroom and I heard the shower turn on. It would have been mean to prevent him from washing, so instead of pushing him for an explanation, I padded into the bathroom, retrieved a toothbrush from the drawer where I kept extra toiletries, and set it on the counter.

"There's a toothbrush next to the sink," I said, trying not to look at his form behind the steamy glass enclosure. "Everything else you need should be in the shower."

"Thanks, Samuel." When I didn't move, he chuckled and spoke again. "I promise I won't be long. Go to bed before you fall over where you're standing."

I was tired beyond belief, but I doubted I'd be able to sleep with everything going on. I was far too anxious. Still, I did what Korban asked and slid between the sheets.

Though I remained awake, the sounds of him in the adjoining room lulled me into a relaxed state instead of making me tense. Even the water turning off, his bare feet slapping on the tile floor, and him brushing his teeth melted tension from me. By the time Korban walked into the bedroom, I was breathing easier and no longer felt ice-cold inside.

"You look better," he said quietly, pressing his palm to my forehead and then brushing my hair back. "Still tired, but better."

I blinked my eyes open and watched him, trying to figure out what he was doing. He was being nice, tender. It didn't make sense. And I liked it, which also didn't make sense.

"A good night's sleep and you'll be back to yourself."

"Why are you doing this?" I said quietly. "I hurt you and you're taking care of me. Why?"

"For the same reason I'm going to get in bed with you and you're going to let me."

"There are lots of other bedrooms in this house," I said. "The beds are just as comfortable. The doors have locks."

Not that I couldn't break through a locked door, but at least it would be some barrier to keep him safe from me.

"I know." He picked up the blanket and sat down. The man had no self-preservation instinct.

I looked at him for a second and then slid to the side, making room for him to lie next to me.

Immediately, he reached over, wrapped his arms around me, and tugged me close until we were pressed together. It was then I remembered he was nude. It made sense because he hadn't been wearing clothes before the shower and he didn't have any at my house. But still, he was nude. In my bed.

"What?" he asked.

"I didn't say anything."

"Your entire body tensed and you're barely breathing." He smiled and combed his fingers through my hair. I had never let anyone touch me that way, not even my parents. But I let him. I liked it. "That's saying something with your body. What freaked you out?"

"You're not wearing any clothes."

"I know."

"Oh." I swallowed hard, thinking about his nonresponse. "Why aren't you wearing any clothes?"

"For the same reason you're glad I'm not wearing any clothes."

I had no idea what he meant. I wasn't glad he was nude. Well, I may have liked it, but that was because I wasn't right in the head. I'd proven that with what I'd done to him.

"Aren't you scared I'm going to hurt you?" I asked.

"No." He shook his head and continued stroking my hair.

"Why not?"

"For the same reason I'm not wearing clothes, you're in your underpants, and we're both enjoying it." He raised himself on his elbow and cupped my cheek. "For the same reason you let me in your bed." He slowly lowered his face toward mine. "For the same reason you're letting me touch you right now."

My heart raced, my breath came out in fast pants, and despite my exhaustion, my dick hardened.

"I'm touching you, Samuel." He ghosted his lips over my forehead and rubbed his palm across my neck and chest. It was highly intimate, the kind of contact I never would have imagined, let alone allowed. But I didn't want to stop him.

"I don't understand what's happening," I confessed.

"Yes, you do. Stop thinking. Just feel."

Before I could deny his assertion or ask what he meant or explain that using my brain was important, he closed the gap between us and pressed his lips against mine.

The feelings were already there—locked away, hidden, but there. His kiss led them out from the darkness where they were buried and showed them the light of day. He felt so good, so right, touching my face, smoothing his soft lips over mine, teasing my tongue into his mouth and letting me taste him. Before I knew it, I was reaching for him, tangling my fingers in the sides of his hair, and holding on to him, keeping him close, keeping us connected.

Without separating our mouths, he rolled on top of me and wedged himself between my thighs. I whimpered and felt him smile in response. All the while, he kept kissing my lips and petting my face. It was amazing—the warm caress of his skin, his scent surrounding me, the sound of him breathing. For the first time in my life, I was where I was meant to be, who I was meant to be. I was whole.

Gasping, I jerked back and stared at Korban. It wasn't supposed to be possible. It shouldn't have made any sense. And yet, suddenly, everything made sense and anything seemed possible.

"You're my mate," I rasped. "My true mate."

"Yes." He beamed, the sides of his eyes crinkling. He moved his fingertips over my eyebrows, my cheekbones, my nose, my lips, and my jaw while he gazed at me reverently. "And I am so very lucky."

He kissed me again, lightly this time, just a brush of his lips over mine, and then he slid off me, curled his arms around me protectively, and said, "Sleep now. I have you. We'll talk more in the morning."

I knew he was there before I opened my eyes. His strong arms were around me, I was using his shoulder as a pillow, and I had my leg over his hip. I had never rested more soundly and peacefully than I did that night.

"Good morning," I croaked, my voice weak from lack of use.

"I think at this point, we can call it evening."

"Evening?" I rubbed my hands over my eyes. "Really?"

I wanted to look at him, but I was too nervous, so I picked at the sheet instead.

"It's four o'clock," he said. "I'd say that counts as early evening." He brushed my hair back, kissed my forehead, and then tilted my chin up until our eyes met. "You really needed sleep. How do you feel?"

I blinked until I could focus on his face. It was so close and I wanted to kiss him, but I wasn't sure if I was allowed to.

"You're my mate," he said. "Of course you're allowed to kiss me."

I hadn't meant to say that out loud.

"Would it make you feel better if I kissed you instead?"

My brain was short-circuiting from the knowledge that I was in bed with someone. That the someone was a male was particularly odd, but truly, it wasn't the biggest reason for my anxiety. I had never kissed anyone before the previous night, and the few touches I had endured were either affection given by my parents or attempts at seduction by females; none of those involved my bare skin and none had lasted more than a few seconds. So everything about my current position—lying in bed tangled with a man, having nothing more than one pair of underwear between us, feeling him caress me and wanting to push into the touch instead of run away from it—was completely outside the scope of my life experiences. And yet Korban seemed perfectly comfortable, completely at ease.

Narrowing my eyes at him, I sat up. "Why are you so casual about this?"

He tilted his head to the side and furrowed his brow in confusion. "I'm not sure what you mean."

"This. Us." I pointed back and forth between us. "We slept together. All night. We were in bed. Touching and holding. Last night we kissed. You're naked right now." I pointed to the sheet covering his groin. "Under there, you're naked and I was just under there, so your, uh, you know was pressed against me."

"I still don't... What?"

"How is it you're calm and collected about all this?" I squeaked. "Are you used to it? Is that it? Are you used to taking off your clothes and climbing in bed with people?"

His frown smoothed into a grin. "Oh, I see." He covered my tightly closed fists with his hands. "You're jealous."

That was completely ridiculous. I had never been jealous of anything. Jealousy was a weak emotion; it didn't portray strength and confidence. Alphas were not jealous.

"I am not jealous," I huffed. "I am merely listing facts."

"Listing facts?" he repeated with a chuckle.

"Yes." I crossed my arms over my chest, trying to look calm and authoritative. It wasn't easy to pull off while almost naked. "I can't help but notice how easy this has been for you. And I know how friendly you are. I've heard about you."

"Heard about me?" He pressed his lips together, like he was holding back laughter.

"Yes. You were the presumptive Alpha of a neighboring pack. It was my duty to learn about you. I heard all about how you were shiny, happy, friendly, and beloved." I paused when my chest grumbled involuntarily. "How friendly and beloved were you?"

Without warning, Korban shot up, clutched my shoulders, and tackled me onto my back. He crouched above me, his knees on either side of my thighs, and grinned.

"I'm tempted to string this out so I can see how much you want to keep me to yourself, but I can't do that to you." He squeezed my shoulders. "You're my true mate, Samuel. True mates are made to be together. I could never want to share anyone's bed but yours."

"What about before you knew I was your mate?" I asked, thinking of all the nights I'd traveled to other regions' meetings searching for someone to tie with. Had Korban done the same thing? Had he succeeded?

"I knew when I was eleven, honey," he said gently, moving one hand from my shoulder to the side of my neck. "I have known who you were to me from the moment I first saw you."

I loved hearing him call me his honey, loved that he thought of me that way. I loved how he touched me, how tender he was, how natural it felt. I loved the way he looked at me like I was precious to him. I loved the soft tenor of his voice when he spoke to me.

I loved all those things so much that I was momentarily distracted from what he'd said. "Eleven?" I said the instant my brain processed his words. "You knew all the way back then?"

Tapping his chest, he nodded. "I felt it."

Looking back, I had felt something too, but there was no way I could have recognized it for what it was. Everything I had learned stood in direct conflict with that possibility. But Korban had learned the same things. The teachings didn't change from pack to pack; the writings were the same.

"You must think me such a fool," I said, ashamed. "You knew as a child. I'm twenty-three years old."

"You're not a fool. You're strong and educated. You believe in pack history and traditions."

"And you don't?"

He shrugged nonchalantly, as if we weren't discussing the rules governing both of our lives. "Yoram Smith, one of my closest friends, has an uncle with a male true mate." He brushed his lips over each of my eyebrows. "I've known Ethan since I was a young child, so I realized it could happen."

"How is it I've never heard about this or read about it?" I asked, my voice pitching high with surprise and frustration at yet another of my failings. "Miancarem is our neighboring pack. I learned about the pack, about its history, about—"

"Yoram's uncle hasn't been a member of our pack in generations."

"Generations?" I asked. "How old is he?"

"He's mated to a vampire, so he's, well, if not immortal, something close to it," Korban said.

My jaw dropped. "A shifter is mated to a vampire?" My entire world order was changing at a disturbingly rapid clip.

"Yes. My great-grandfather was Alpha when they ran Ethan out of the pack. They considered him an abomination and a shame, so they didn't write about him or tell anyone about him. But his family didn't turn their backs on him. They're quiet about it, but he comes to visit. He stays off pack lands in the human town, and his family goes to see him. I went with Yoram as a child—that's how I know Ethan and Miguel."

"I'm sorry." I was so ashamed. "You knew we were mates. All that time you knew, and I was terrible to you." Thinking about how I'd treated Korban made me sick. "And you tried to be nice to me." I paused and thought about it. "You were nice and I was horrible, and then when they brought you here, I...I hurt you so much."

"No." Korban grasped my chin, holding me still. His blue eyes blazed. "You have never hurt me."

"But I made you—"

"You didn't make me do anything I haven't wanted to do nearly every day for well over a decade."

Korban's cheeks reddened and he ducked his head, looking shy for the first time since I'd known him.

"Korban?" I asked.

"I told him about you," he said quietly. "You remember that day when we saw each other at the regional meeting and you were late because of the car accident?"

That day was impossible to forget, and I felt my cheeks heat too. "Uh-huh."

"I knew what had happened. I could smell you. The way your face looked." He trembled and sucked in a deep breath. "I was fifteen, so I knew a fair bit about how males and females tied, but I wasn't sure how we'd do it. I begged Yoram to tell me the next time Ethan came to visit. At first he said no because the last time his family took me, my father found out and made sure they suffered for it. But I was old enough to get there on my own and he trusted that I'd never say he had any part of it, so a few months later, when his uncle came, Yoram told me. I snuck off pack lands, went to Ethan's hotel, and asked him about tying with a male. After that, it was all I could think about." He gazed into my eyes. "I could have stopped you anytime." He must have sensed my disbelief, because he kept talking. "Did I ask you to stop?"

Hesitantly, I shook my head.

"See? If I had asked you to stop, you would have."

It was a nice thought, but it wasn't true, and I couldn't lie to him. "No. You don't understand. I lost control of my form. I couldn't think straight."

"You tied with your mate, Samuel," he said firmly. "That was instinct, and though it certainly could have been more romantic, you were doing what we both needed and wanted." He paused and looked at me meaningfully. "Not just what you needed, but what both of us needed."

"I didn't know you were my mate," I confessed. "I realize that makes me a fool. You knew as a child. Shifters are supposed to recognize their true mates. But I'd always learned that males have to tie with females, and I never considered... I never thought..."

"Intellectually, you didn't know. That's true. You're so smart, Samuel." He beamed, looking proud of that fact. "And I think maybe because you're so smart, you forget there's more to knowledge than what's up here." He tapped my head. "Your wolf half is more driven by instinct, by your gut. In that form, you recognized who I am to you, so that form took over. Stop punishing yourself for following your instincts. The same instincts will always stop you from hurting me. If I had asked you to stop, you would have."

"Do you really believe that?" I whispered, desperately wanting it to be true. I didn't want to cause Korban pain, not ever.

"I know it."

"I didn't hurt you?"

"No." He shook his head. "I suspect it'll feel better if we slow down next time and use some lubrication, but my mate—my brilliant, always composed, always careful, always prepared mate—wanted me so much he couldn't think." He cupped my cheek. "If there's one thing I know about you, Samuel Goodwin, it's that your brain is constantly running, evaluating, considering. But it wasn't then, was it? When we were in that workshop and you—"

I winced at what he was about to say, but he held my gaze and continued.

"When you tied with me and gave me the mating bite, you weren't thinking. For what I strongly suspect was the first time in your life, you followed your gut, your body." He paused. "You followed your heart. Because of me." He smiled broadly, the sides of his eyes crinkling and his face lighting up. "No, honey, that didn't hurt."

CHAPTER 12

I HAD A lot to think about, including whether I thought too much. But one thing was at the forefront.

"What about you?" I asked. "Do I ever make you, uh, not think?" I gulped and darted my gaze away, feeling too exposed by the conversation to reveal any other part of me.

"Are you asking if I want you?" Korban said, his voice going husky. He spread his legs and slid down over me, grinding his erection against my hip. "Does that answer your question?"

Suddenly breathless and ramrod hard, I nodded.

He settled on top of me and nuzzled my throat. "I want to bite you," he whispered. "I want to push myself deep into your body, lock you to me, and mate."

I whimpered, his words arousing me uncontrollably despite knowing that what he wanted would be uncomfortable for me. It didn't matter. I had taken what I needed from him twice, and he hadn't complained. Korban needed to tie—my mate needed to tie—and I would give that to him.

"Okay," I said, my voice shaky. "You can do that to me." With him lying on me, it wasn't easy, but I managed to wiggle out of my underwear and flip over. When my belly was pressed against the mattress and my backside was accessible to him, I said, "Go ahead."

Waiting for him to begin, I squeezed my eyes shut and gripped the sheets. He didn't do as I expected and push his prick into me. Instead, he kissed the back of my neck.

"Korban?"

"Uh-huh?" He kissed me again, swiping his tongue out that time and licking my nape.

"What are you doing?"

"Kissing you." He followed the explanation with a series of kisses from my hairline to the top of my spine. "Tasting you." He licked and sucked his way across my shoulder. "Touching you." He smoothed his fingers down my flank, sensitizing my skin. "Making love to you."

"I don't understand."

Korban wrapped his arms around me, squeezed me tight, and then wedged his face against the side of my neck and laughed. "Only you," he said.

"Only me what?"

"I'll make you a deal—" He kissed my cheek. "Let me do this my way. Try your best to put your active mind on pause and feel. If you still don't understand afterward, I'll explain it to you."

It was a reasonable request. Besides, I had already committed myself to letting him do whatever he needed. He was my mate; it was my duty to take care of him and meet his needs. Tying was one of those needs. Thinking of it in those terms eased me. I wanted to provide for my mate in whatever way I could.

"Okay," I said as I settled onto the mattress again.

"I'll be right back." He kissed my shoulder and climbed off the bed.

I waited calmly, ready for whatever came, wanting to fulfill him.

In moments, he was back, straddling me again. "Remember the night you came to Miancarem for the young adults meeting?" he whispered in my ear. Before I could answer, he breathed his way down the back of my neck. "I wanted to do this to you then." He kissed my vertebrae, one by one.

"Why didn't you?" I asked.

He rested his cheek against my lower back and squeezed me tight. "You never would have let me. You didn't recognize who I was to you."

"You could have told me," I said defensively. "Why didn't you?"

"Believe me, I thought about it, but I was trying to deal with my father and my uncle. They're stubborn, set in their ways. I had to get my pack in order."

I wanted to ask what he meant about his pack, but I sensed he wasn't done talking, so I waited.

"Besides, you wouldn't have believed me back then. You were so skittish with me, so hesitant to trust me. If I'd told you I was your mate, you would have heard me with your head and dismissed it as not matching what you already thought to be facts about mating."

Cupping my backside with both hands, he dug his fingers into the muscles and rubbed hard. I gasped in surprise before moaning contentedly. Without stopping, Korban brushed his lips over the small of my back.

"The only way for you to recognize me as your mate was for you to feel it in your heart, in your soul." Keeping a firm grip on my ass, he moved his hands to the sides, which spread me open. "Your mind is so strong, Samuel." His breath warmed the exposed skin in my channel, and I shuddered. "I was worried you'd never feel for me enough to break through it."

Before I could think about what he said and consider the truth of it, he ran his tongue from the small of my back all the way to my balls, and my mind short-circuited.

"Korban," I gasped.

"So good," he said hoarsely before licking his way back up my channel. "Want you." He continued to work me over with his mouth, focusing on a progressively smaller area. "Need you." He flicked his tongue over my puckered opening, and I cried out at the unexpected delight. "Yes, let me hear you."

He licked faster for a few moments and then changed tactics. Instead of using his warm, slick tongue to bring me pleasure from the outside, he pressed it to my opening and smoothly slid it inside my body.

"Oh God, Korban."

Continuing to flick his tongue, he swiped it against the sensitive skin inside my hole before pulling it out and then pushing it back in. His sounds of pleasure melded with mine, both of us moaning as we joined together in harsh, raw intimacy.

"Yes," I cried out, tilting my hips up in an attempt to get closer to his talented mouth. "Please."

"Hold yourself open," Korban rasped.

Scrambling to comply so he would keep his mouth on me and his tongue in me, I rested my weight on my shoulders, kept my ass raised, and held my cheeks open. "Like this?" I asked.

"I never thought..." He whimpered low and long. "I didn't dare let myself hope you'd be this way with me." I felt him shiver behind me before he pressed his soft lips against my opening. "Thank you for trusting me. I'll never take it for granted."

So far immersed in the passion he inspired within me, my mind was slow to process his words. And then he distracted me further by reaching between my legs and taking my dick in hand just as he lowered his mouth and resumed pleasuring my insides with his tongue.

"Ungh," I groaned. My mouth gaped, and I sucked in air as I felt sharp pulls in my groin. "Korban."

He stroked my dick faster and pumped his tongue in and out of my hole. I had never felt so good.

"Thank you. Please. More," I babbled as I rocked between Korban's hot mouth and his tight grip. "I'm going to." Throwing my head back, I gasped and then stopped breathing. "Going to—"

I came before I could complete the sentence, seed pulsing from my cock in powerful bursts. The orgasm felt like it lasted forever, and by the time my balls finished emptying, I was drained in every way.

"Korban," I said hoarsely. Needing to see his beautiful face, I gathered all my strength and flipped onto my back.

Immediately, he moved up until we were eye-to-eye and then he peppered kisses all over my face, caressed me, and gazed at me with heat and joy and affection. I felt cherished. There was no other way to describe it.

"You taste so good," he said.

Though I couldn't form words, I communicated by reaching between us and gently running my fingers over his shaft. He was still hard and I wanted to satisfy him.

"I'm not done," he explained. After taking another kiss that left my lungs heaving, he scooted down my body and began playing with my balls.

With any other person, I surely wouldn't have allowed access to the most vulnerable part of my body, but when Korban cupped me in his warm hand, I simply spread my legs farther and sighed in pleasure.

"You're beautiful, Samuel," he whispered. "Every part of you." Gently, he moved his thumb back and forth over the top of my testicles while at the same time he lifted them and pressed his fingertips against my perineum. "Do you know that I've never seen anyone with cheekbones like yours? I searched. Really. I'd see you and notice how sharp and high they are, and then for years after, I'd stare at every new person who crossed my path, looking to see if they had those defined cheekbones, but nobody ever did.

"And your eyes." He groaned, lowered his face to my groin, and licked my sac. "You're so cool, so calm, so fierce. Nothing riles you up, so it's impossible to know how you're feeling. But when I watched really close, I started noticing things." He mouthed one testicle, closing and opening his lips over it. "When you're upset, your eyes get so light, the green bleeds out of them until they look silver." He moved to the other testicle and took it between his lips, suckling gently. "And when you're happy, the green darkens to the shade of spring grass." He looked at me from between my legs. "Like now." With his gaze locked on mine, he swiped his tongue up my shaft and then circled it around my glans. "You're happy, right?"

I nodded, swallowed hard, and said, "Yes."

"Good." He graced me with one of his smiles, a serene one, and rubbed his cheek down the length of my shaft. "Mmm," he moaned, his eyes drooping shut as he continued to slide my cock all over his face.

I gasped and bucked at the eroticism of his action. "Korban."

He opened his eyes and looked at me. "Uh-huh."

"Can you... Will you...?" I bit my lower lip.

"Say it, honey. Say what you want from me. I'll give it to you. Always."

"Suck me," I whispered.

He smiled, his eyes bright. "With pleasure."

After dragging his lips up the length of my dick, he swirled his tongue on my heated skin. When he got to the crown, he parted his lips and dropped down, taking me in.

"Oh!" I cried out at the sensation of wet suction. "Oh!"

Rumbling happily, he sucked me farther inside, tightened his lips around me, and then slid up before sucking me down again. He clutched my hips tightly, holding me still as he made me soar. I curled my palms over his head and held on as he bobbed up and down. All the while, our gazes remained locked together, elevating the intimacy of the moment almost unbearably.

I felt completely exposed, like those blue eyes were peering into my head, into my soul, like he could see everything. Still, I couldn't look away, couldn't break the connection; I didn't want to. Korban could have any part of me.

"I want to be inside you," he said as he swiped his tongue down the length of my erection. "I want to feel you all around me." He nuzzled my testicles.

"Yes," I said quietly, desperately wanting the same thing.

"Hand me that lotion." He tipped his forehead toward the nightstand, and I turned to find a bottle of lotion I normally kept in my bathroom. I was meticulous about maintaining everything in its place, so I was thrown off for a moment. "I brought it in," Korban said, apparently sensing my confusion. "It'll make everything smoother and more comfortable."

While he spoke, he rubbed his fingertip around my puckered skin, exerting a hint of pressure. Wanting more, I grabbed the lotion and handed it to him.

"Thanks, honey." Keeping his finger in place, he dipped his face and ran his tongue around the outside of my hole.

"Korban," I moaned. "Feels good."

Closing his eyes, he took in a deep breath. When he opened them again, his lips tilted upward. "Always," he promised. After kissing my thigh, he sat up on his heels, reached for a pillow, and then stuffed it under my backside, elevating my hips. "I want to see your face while we do this." He dragged one hand up my belly and chest. "I want to kiss you when I'm inside."

Everything about the moment was tender and intimate—his quiet voice, the warmth of his touch, the reverence in his expression. There could be no doubt that I mattered to Korban, and I realized for the first time that the way he had looked at me over the years was exactly the same. I hadn't recognized it for what it was, so it had confused me, put me off-balance, but now that I felt his affection, I understood it and I wanted more.

"Will you kiss me now?" I asked.

Without hesitation, he slid up my body, tangled his left hand in my hair, and lowered his lips over mine. The kisses were soft, our lips brushing, his tongue tracing my mouth. And while we moved our mouths together, he probed me with slick fingers, rubbing, circling, and eventually pushing cool lotion inside my passage. I moaned at his touch and spread my legs wider. Taking my invitation, Korban slowly but steadily pushed his finger into my hole.

"Ungh," I moaned as I draped my hands around his neck.

"You're so soft and hot inside," he whispered as he pumped his finger in and out of me.

I dug my hands into his hair, tugged his bottom lip between both of mine, and circled my legs around his hips.

"Mmm, Samuel." After taking another quick kiss, he leaned back, and the smooth, blunt heat of his cockhead prodded my entrance. With his gaze locked on mine, he pushed forward, slowly entering my body.

I had expected it to hurt, but there was no pain, only a feeling of connection and warmth. When he bottomed out, he returned his lips to mine, circling his hips and moaning into my mouth before gliding out again. Meeting his motions, I raised my backside as he entered and pulled back when he slid out. Neither of us moved quickly. We enjoyed the moment, enjoyed the connection, enjoyed each other.

"Just like this," he whispered into my mouth. "From now on we can be just like this."

My heart soared at his words, feeling complete and whole. The constant, steady in and out, the scent of his skin, and the sounds of his body slapping against mine inflamed me further. I tightened my hold on him, grasping his shoulders and digging my heels into his ass, and thrust my hips up and down.

"Oh God," he groaned. "Need you."

As if my passion inspired his, Korban's breath came out faster and he plunged into me harder and deeper. The mating knot at the base of his cock swelled and locked him inside me, keeping us connected. Instinctively, I arched my neck back and to the side.

Mine. I heard the word in my head as he lunged and buried his sharp canines into the juncture of my neck and shoulder. My balls tightened, and my seed burst from me in a perfect moment of bliss. Korban shivered above me as he emptied himself into my body. Mine.

It wasn't until I was spent, gasping for air, and feeling Korban lick the permanent mark he had given me that I realized I'd heard that voice before.

It had led me back from the depths of the forest the day my father died. It had taken me to the evidence that showed the cause of his demise. It had comforted me when the council members had delivered Korban rather than Dirk as my tribute. It had calmed me when my pack member questioned me and I went for his jugular.

"Korban?" I asked shakily.

He kissed my cheek and buried his face against my throat. "My mate," he whispered.

CHAPTER 13

"I HEARD YOU," I said quietly as I gently combed my fingers through his hair. "Just now, in my head and other times too." I cleared my throat. "I heard you, and you helped me when I needed you most."

After his mating knot had receded, he had kissed his way down my torso, lapped up my seed, and then resumed his earlier attention to my groin.

"How did you know about the syringe?" I asked. "You weren't at the battle, but you led me to it."

"I was gone when my father issued the challenge. I hurried back as soon as I could, but it was too late. As soon as I heard what happened, I went to the battle ring to scent you, and that's when I saw it. I knew right away something was wrong. My father is strong, but your father is stronger. So then I looked for you and brought you to it."

"You brought me to it by talking to me in my head," I said.

"It happens with true mates," he said. "That's what I've heard."

"Yes. I've read about it. But the writings say a mental link develops only after true mates have been tying for a long time. That's if it develops at all."

Korban shrugged and went back to licking my balls. "The writings aren't always accurate. I think we've already established that. Besides, we've known each other for fifteen years."

"That's another thing," I said, thinking out loud. "Our ancestors' writings say true mates don't meet in childhood."

Not seeming bothered in the least by yet another inconsistency between what we'd been taught and what we now knew without a doubt to be true, Korban caressed my thigh and said, "Do the writings give a reason?"

"Um." I thought back to what I'd read. "I think it's to prevent people from tying and having cubs too young."

Snickering, Korban said, "Well, I doubt either of us is going to find himself accidently with child." He shook his head. "Isn't it funny how so many of these absolute truths and rules we learn have the added bonus of controlling our behavior to match some old-fashioned sense of right and wrong?"

"I never thought of it that way."

"Well, you're the expert scholar, not me, but it sure seems that way."

I couldn't dispute the truth of that observation. "You're right. Maybe it's time we reevaluate the writings and pack lore."

"You mean ignore?" He waggled his eyebrows and grinned, reminding me of the boy he used to be. I wished I could have seen him then, really seen him, instead of being confused and afraid.

"History is important. Learning about our ancestors helps us know ourselves." I meant those words, believed them completely. But I also believed knowledge was useful only if it was accurate. "The writings can be updated. Shifters no different from you and me wrote those words. What's to stop us from sharing our knowledge with future generations?"

"Nothing."

"I think I'll do it," I said.

"You should. As it stands, a lot of the pack lore was written by closed-minded bigots and now it's being used to control us." He sighed. "Believe me. I've seen it firsthand."

Those words were familiar. I'd heard them very recently. "I spoke with Zev Hassick yesterday." I tugged on Korban's hair and diverted his attention from my cock, which he was lifting as if he was weighing it with his palm. His gentle fondling was causing that weight to increase despite the two earth-shattering orgasms he'd already given me. "He asked how you were doing," I said.

"He knows you're my true mate." Korban wrapped his hand around my shaft, not stroking, just holding on.

"How?"

"I told him." He lowered his mouth and huffed hot air on my sensitive cockhead.

I whimpered.

"I knew you'd contact the interpack council about the syringe, so after I led you there through our mental link, I called Zev, and he called one of his friends on the council. Then when they were struggling with your demand for a tribute, they called him. Some of them are traditionalists, so they had no problem with the idea of following the rules, but some couldn't go along with the idea of sending me to my death because of something I hadn't done."

"I'm so sorry. I—"

"Don't be," Korban said, sounding completely sincere. "You didn't know it was going to be me. You thought you'd get my father, and I don't blame you for wanting him dead. Anyway, Zev's friends on the council called him to discuss what was happening, he called me, and I told him the truth. Once he knew I was your true mate, he told his friends to let the tribute go forward, which was good because from what I hear they were close to imploding over this."

"Why would he tell them to send you to your death?" I asked in confusion. "I thought he was your friend."

"Zev has a true mate. He knows what that means, knows true mates would do anything to protect each other." He gazed up at me, his expression soft, warm, and trusting. "Writings are just words on paper. Feeling half your soul live in another body is real. He realized you'd never hurt me."

Both of us were quiet for a couple of minutes, and then Korban whispered, "Samuel?"

"Yes?"

"I'm sorry about your father. He was a great man. I always admired him."

I nodded, too choked up to speak.

"I never would have stood by and let my father challenge him if I had known about it."

"That's why Dirk, uh, your father insisted on the challenge happening so quickly? He wanted you to miss it."

"I think so, yeah," Korban said. "That and because he was afraid of losing control of the pack."

"What do you mean?"

"I'm twenty-six," Korban said. "I'm old enough to take over as Alpha. A lot of people in the pack aren't happy with my father." He scoffed. "Hell, they weren't happy with his predecessor, either. I've heard grumbling about my grandfather and his father. Anyway, lots of people want him out, but if someone challenges him, pack members would have to take sides, which means fracturing the pack. For several years now, the contingent that doesn't like my father has been biding their time, waiting for him to hand over the reins to me."

"They trust you," I said, pride bubbling up inside me at the knowledge that my mate was a good man, respected by his pack.

"The ones who know me really well trust me, but I'm still a Keller, so the rest of them were willing to give me the benefit of the doubt only because they trusted their family and friends who know me." Korban shook his head. "Unfortunately, my father doesn't want to let go of his power. From what I heard, he thought showing up your father and taking over the Yafenack pack would improve his standing within the Miancarem pack, which is ridiculous because it's exactly the type of mindless, aggressive behavior that created the rift."

"My father used to say lowering those around us doesn't improve us." I remembered those lessons and so many others he had taught me, and though I'd never get over losing him, I was comforted by the realization that he lived within me, and I could still make him proud by carrying on his message.

"Your father was a strong shifter and a strong leader." Korban kissed my belly. "You're going to follow in his footsteps."

"I want to do right by my pack. It's all I've ever wanted. For a long time, I wasn't sure I'd be able to do it because I had problems shifting into my human form." I looked away, still uncomfortable with the reason that problem had resolved itself.

Korban, on the other hand, had no qualms talking about it. He scooted up the bed until he was next to me. "But that got better after you tied with me, right?"

"Yes." I nodded. "But I've never been as good with people as my father." I took in a deep breath and confessed my biggest fear. "I worry I'll never measure up and the pack will suffer."

Korban cupped my cheek and traced my bottom lip with his thumb. "Don't sell yourself short. You're respected far and wide for your knowledge of pack lore and history. Everyone describes you as brilliant and calm under pressure. After the way you battled with my father, I'm sure word will spread of your wolf's strength."

I rolled onto my side, wrapped my arm around his waist, wedged my leg between his thighs, and tucked my head under his chin, connecting us as closely as possible. My whole life I had fidgeted when anybody got too near, and there I was trying to bury myself under Korban's skin.

"And as far as being good with people, you said I'm friendly and beloved." My face heated at the reminder of my poorly hidden jealousy. Thankfully, he couldn't see my face. "We're mates, which means I'll be by your side every step of the way, helping fill any gaps." He brushed his fingers through my hair. "You're not doing this alone."

Both of us had worked up an appetite in bed, so while Korban called Zev Hassick to let him know he was doing well, I went downstairs to make us food.

"Whatcha cookin', good-lookin'?" Korban playfully asked as he walked into the kitchen and set my phone on the counter.

He wore an old pair of my sweatpants but no shirt, which bared his defined chest and distracted me. Blinking, I stared at the mouthwatering sight before me, the tongs in my hand forgotten.

Not waiting for an answer, he stepped up behind me, wrapped his arms around my waist, and looked over my shoulder at the four large cuts of meat sizzling in the grill pan. "Mmm, steak. It looks great." He inhaled deeply. "Smells great too." He patted my backside. "So what are you having?" He walked toward the fridge.

"Just kidding. I can share my meat with you." He barely had the sentence out before he started cracking up like a teenager.

Korban was smiling, sounding happy, joking around. It was like we were friends. I'd never had a friend, so I didn't know for sure, but it felt that way. I really liked it.

"I, uh, made fries too," I said. "They're in the oven."

"Steak and fries?"

He moaned and rubbed his belly, drawing my eye to the muscles there and the V-shaped lines leading down to his groin. It was a challenge to raise my gaze.

"Those are two of my favorite things," he said. "You're spoiling me."

Ducking my head, I blinked at the praise.

Within seconds, he was back at my side, handing me a glass of water. When I took it, he kissed my neck. "You already have my heart. You don't need to bribe my stomach."

Though I wasn't sure how to respond to his never-ending stream of affection and sweetness, I adored it. "I'm not bribing. I want to take care of you," I whispered before gulping down the water.

With a soft smile, Korban took the tongs and flipped the steaks over. "That works out well because I want to take care of you too." After looking at me for another few seconds, he sighed contentedly and then turned off the burner. "I'll get some plates." He tilted his chin toward the steaks. "Those are done."

Korban found the silverware drawer and got us forks and knives while I plated the steak and fries.

"What did Zev Hassick say?" I asked after we'd made sizable dents in our food.

"He congratulated me on our mating, said from what he'd heard about you and what he knew about me, we'd be well matched, and told me my Uncle Dennis took over as Alpha of Miancarem despite the speculation."

"What speculation?"

Scrunching his eyebrows together, Korban paused with his fork inches from his mouth. "Dennis was one of the witnesses to the challenge."

"I know. I scented him."

His frown smoothed away. "You scented him across the battle ring with the smells of the forest and the other witnesses around you, and you recognized him as my father's brother?"

I nodded.

"That's amazing." Korban pushed his plate aside, reached over the table, covered my hand with his, and squeezed it. "You're such a strong shifter, Samuel."

When I was younger, I was sure I'd be the strongest Alpha in the history of any pack. But in the intervening years, I'd experienced enough limitations to curb that youthful exuberance, or maybe it was arrogance. Either way, I had gotten to the point where I worried I wouldn't be fit to be a member of a pack, let alone lead one. It seemed that mating with Korban remedied those shortcomings, but I was still adjusting to the idea.

For that reason, I looked at my plate, cleared my throat, and said, "So, uh, you mentioned something about speculation?"

"My uncle and my father are really tight. I wasn't at the challenge, so I'm not sure how everything went down, but I wouldn't be surprised if Dennis had a part in it."

Reflecting back on the day my father was killed, I realized Korban was probably right. Though it would have been possible for Dirk to have hidden the syringe in the brush in advance, it wasn't likely. His witnesses had been right next to the ring when my father landed on him and he shifted. It wasn't far-fetched to imagine someone handing Dirk the syringe or even injecting the drug himself during the commotion.

"That's possible," I said. "It would have been hard for Dirk to have done it on his own."

"Exactly." Korban nodded and sighed in frustration. "But there's no way to prove anyone else was involved, and even if someone was, there's no way to prove it was Dennis. That's why the interpack council can't touch him no matter how much they suspect he had a part in it."

The possessive nature of Alphas and the strong sense of pack pride in members meant pack governance rested within the pack. The interpack council got involved only in rare and extreme circumstances, and even then, the council limited their role as much as possible. Doing otherwise would risk drawing the ire of the entire pack and even other packs, who would worry about their own control being usurped.

The situation surrounding Dirk's challenge of my father had already stretched the limits of the council's role beyond what they normally did—they had unseated one Alpha and handed over another as a tribute. Stepping in and questioning a third Alpha would be too much, especially with nothing but speculation as a reason. But that didn't explain why the pack would want a man like that to lead them.

"I'm surprised pack members want him as Alpha," I said. "Having an Alpha with that kind of cloud around him diminishes the pack. Besides, your uncle is well past the age of a newly inducted Alpha."

"You're right." Korban frowned. "It doesn't make sense, does it?"

I shook my head. "No, it doesn't." Protecting the pack, bettering the pack, caring for the pack—those goals had been ingrained in me since birth. Apparently they extended beyond the boundaries of my own pack, because I found myself worrying about the Miancarem shifters. "I think you need to find out what's going on. Your pack might be in trouble."

"I'll make some calls," he agreed. "But Miancarem isn't my pack. Not anymore."

My stomach dropped. I had done that. I had yanked Korban from his home and his position. I had put an entire pack at risk because of my ill-planned thirst for vengeance. Too ashamed to meet his eyes, I looked away.

"Stop." Korban grasped my chin and returned my focus to him. "Whatever you're thinking right now, stop. What I meant was you're my mate and Yafenack is your pack. That means it's my pack now too. Like I said earlier, honey, I'll be by your side from here on out."

"But you were Alpha. You'd been waiting for so long, and I—"

"No. I was Alpha because my father was an idiot, but I hadn't been waiting for it."

"What do you mean?" I asked, feeling lost. "You've always been the presumptive Alpha of Miancarem. Everyone knows that. And you said pack members were waiting for your father to step down so you could take his spot."

"All true." He nodded. "But what people thought and what I wanted weren't the same." Korban sighed. "The only thing I've been waiting for is you." His lips tilted up a smidge. "From the moment I saw you and realized who you were to me, I knew I had to figure out how to be with you. That's what I've been planning for the last fifteen years, not how to be Alpha of my pack."

"How to be with me," I repeated quietly.

"Yes. You were going to lead the Yafenack pack. Even when you were eight, I knew it. You were so serious, so focused." He smiled softly. "So damn cute." He shook his head as if to clear it. "Anyway, I knew you'd be Alpha here and I knew I was your mate, so I had no intention of taking over for my father long-term. But I needed you to feel it and I needed to figure out what it would mean for us because of the whole male shifter, female shifter lore."

"Lore?" I said, repeating his word for no discernable reason. I knew what he meant.

"Uh-huh. But that stopped being as big an issue when Zev Hassick mated with a male. I mean, people will still question us and some of them will probably get angry, but once I found out about him, I knew we'd have an easier time."

"And what was your plan before you heard about Zev?"

Korban grinned. "I was going to trust my mate."

I arched my eyebrows in question.

With a shrug, Korban said, "I couldn't come up with a solution, but I figured once you felt who I was to you, you'd use your big brain and all your knowledge about our history and lore to make sure people understood."

I wanted so much to be the shifter he thought I was, but I hadn't proven myself worthy of that kind of trust. "You put a lot of faith in me considering my brain didn't realize you were my true mate for all those years," I whispered hoarsely.

"You have a brilliant mind, don't doubt that." He flipped my hand over and gently ran his fingers over my palm. "So brilliant that maybe sometimes your brain takes up all the available space and doesn't leave room for what you have in here." He rubbed my chest.

My father had tried to tell me a version of that time and again, but I had never truly understood. Yet, hearing Korban say the words made the lightbulb go on, and I finally realized what my shortcomings had been in relating to my pack. At first, I wondered at that. After all, my father had been an excellent communicator. And then it hit me—there was no way to understand what it was to feel.

When my father had taught me, I hadn't had a frame of reference for the kind of emotional connection he wanted me to form with my pack. He had tried over and over; he had used every word possible, all to no avail. It was akin to describing the color yellow to someone who had been born without sight—all the descriptions in the world wouldn't solve the riddle. But finally I understood.

"Korban?" I pushed my chair back, walked over to him, and dropped to my knees. "I think some new room opened up in here." I took his hand and laid it on my chest. "I can feel you."

That was an understatement. Where once I hadn't had emotions to match the words I'd heard, I found myself feeling so deeply, so viscerally, so completely for the man in front of me, that no words were powerful enough to describe the all-encompassing emotion. I wanted him to know. I needed to show him that my years of confusion were behind us. Actions would express what I couldn't find a way to say. Trembling from the inferno raging within me, I placed my hand on his groin and gazed up at him.

His breath hitching and nostrils flaring, Korban spread his legs to make room for me.

I knelt between his thighs, tucked my fingers under his waistband, and waited for him to lift his backside before tugging his pants low enough to expose his thick cock and velvety sac. "Mmm, love how you smell," I whispered as I buried my face in his groin. I lapped at his balls, groaning as his taste, scent, and heat washed over me.

"Samuel, honey," he gasped breathlessly as he grappled with the sides of the chair and then grabbed the table, seemingly not knowing where to put his hands.

Seeing him lose control from the pleasure I gave him caused my cock to swell. I licked my lips and then mouthed my way up his shaft, darting my tongue out as I went, leaving him slick with my saliva. By the time I reached his glans, he was panting and shaking, clenching and releasing his fists, and whimpering.

Swiping my tongue over his slit, I closed my eyes in ecstasy at the taste of him. Blindly, I reached for his hand and dragged it over to my head, letting him know he could let go and take what he needed.

Immediately, he cried out, tangled his fingers in my hair, and thrust his hips up, pushing his dick into my mouth. I never would have imagined that letting someone else use my body and control my movements would be arousing, but with my mate, it was. I enjoyed giving myself to him just as much as I enjoyed taking what he offered me.

With Korban moaning and thrusting above me, I wrapped one hand around the base of his cock, parted my lips wider, and took him as deep as I could. The taste of his skin on my tongue, the stretch of my lips around his girth, and the heat of his erection in my mouth ramped up my arousal. Though my own dick was hungry for attention, I ignored it in favor of pleasuring my mate, using one hand to stroke his cock in time with my mouth and the other to cup and roll his balls.

"I'm close," he warned just as drops of early seed spilled on my tongue.

Humping the air with no touch to my cock, my entire body stiffened, and I came with a muffled moan.

"Did you just… Oh, hell, you did, didn't you?" Grasping my hair almost hard enough to hurt, he growled, bucked his hips, and shoved his dick as far as he could before shooting down my throat.

For several seconds, he kept his firm hold on me, seeming to be locked in bliss. When he eventually slumped back into the chair, he relaxed his fingers and stroked my head. "Sorry," he panted. "Did I hurt you?"

After taking another lick, I released his cock and wiped the back of my hand across my mouth. "No." I shook my head, glanced down at the wetness seeping through my pants, and then raised my gaze. "I'd say I liked that a whole lot."

"You're so sexy," he said hoarsely. He combed his fingers through my hair. "And that was amazing."

I rested my cheek against his leg and sighed in satisfaction. "Yeah, it was."

"Oh," Korban gasped.

"Hmm?" I said as I glanced up at him.

"You're smiling." He traced his fingers over my lips. "I've never seen you smile."

It wasn't something I did often. But I was content and happy through and through, so it made sense that my body was showing it.

"Thank you." I closed my eyes and leaned on him. He stroked the back of my head and massaged my nape. "Mmm," I moaned, my muscles going slack. Everything but Korban disappeared as I reveled in the waves of peace lapping in my mind. "I love you," I mumbled, my tongue feeling thick and heavy. "So much."

CHAPTER 14

THE SUN hadn't yet set when the doorbell rang. Korban and I had gone for a run in our wolf forms, and he was still washing up.

"Someone's at the door," I said as I buttoned my pants and shoved my feet into a pair of loafers. He was a smidge taller than me, but otherwise we had similar builds. A few of my jeans or pants were sure to fit him. "Go ahead and grab anything you want from the closet when you're done."

"Will do," he answered and reached for a bottle of shampoo. The position highlighted the width of his shoulders, narrowness of his waist, and curve of his ass.

My breath hitched, my jaw dropped, and I whimpered at the gorgeous vision before me. I could have derived hours of entertainment from watching his body through the glass.

Unfortunately, the doorbell rang again, reminding me that I was Alpha and pack members were entitled to my attention. Even if it meant missing the sight of my mate wet and sudsy.

With a resigned sigh, I pulled my shirt on and walked out of the bedroom. "Coming," I yelled as I neared the entryway. "Be right there."

I opened the door to find my father's friend Walter Clemson waiting.

"Walter, hi," I said as I stepped back and raised my arm toward the inside of the house. "Please come in."

"Hello, uh, thank you." Walter blinked rapidly, looking confused.
Once he stepped past me, I shut the door, put my hand on his
back, and led him toward the living room. "What can I do for you?"
He reared back in response to my touch.

"Are you okay?" I asked, worried he was injured and I hadn't
realized.

"I'm fine." He stared at me. "Just fine." He cleared his throat. "Are
you?"

"Yes. Thank you." Something was clearly bothering him, so I
smiled, trying to put him at ease. "Can I get you anything to drink?"

"No." He shook his head. "I'm fine."

His body language didn't match his assertion, but I let it go,
figuring he'd explain what he needed soon enough. "Have a seat,"
I said and then sat on the couch, rested my forearms on my knees,
and waited for him to get settled.

"What's going on with you?" he asked hesitantly. "You're acting
strange."

"Strange?" I mentally reflected on my behavior over the previous
couple of minutes, but nothing about it seemed out of the ordinary.

"Maybe not strange, exactly, but you're not acting like yourself.
You touched my back. You seem pleased to see me here even though
I didn't call first or make an appointment. You smiled." He breathed
out heavily. "Are you sure nothing's going on?"

There was a time when I might have taken offense at that
statement or become defensive, but I knew better. Walter was right.
Only days earlier, I would have cringed if anyone had touched me,
and yet I had touched him without a second thought. Smiling to put
a pack member at ease had come instinctively, but it was unusual
for me; Korban had said the same thing. But though I was behaving
differently, I was still being myself—a better version of myself.

"A lot has happened these past few days," I admitted, choosing my words carefully. I wanted to tell him about my mate, but I hadn't yet charted out a plan for revealing the information. That announcement was too important to be tossed out without careful thought.

"Right. Yes." He nodded. "That's why I'm here. I heard from my son that there are issues with the tribute."

"Issues?" I bit out, using every ounce of control I had to keep myself from flying into a rage at the way he referred to my mate as if he were a thing instead of a person.

"Yes." He gulped and tensely said, "Did you kill him yet?"

Involuntarily, I growled deep in my chest, curled my lips to bare my teeth, and squeezed my fists so tightly my knuckles cracked. The mere mention of Korban being hurt would have been enough to ignite my fury; hearing his death referred to so nonchalantly was maddening. But the fault for his question lay at my feet—I was the one who had demanded retribution for my father's murder.

Forcing myself to relax my shoulders and close my eyes, I let the anger pass as much as possible. When I was calm enough to treat my pack member well, I looked at him again.

"No," I said. "Korban isn't dead."

If it was possible, Walter looked more uncomfortable. "Jason said Rick Collins tricked him into coming here and—" He cleared his throat and focused on a spot over my shoulder instead of looking me in the eyes. "He said the tribute—"

"Korban."

Walter arched his eyebrows in question.

"His name is Korban Keller," I said, pleased I'd managed to keep my voice free of anger. "And that's right. Rick and Jason were here yesterday." Assuming Walter had come to discuss his son's injuries,

I said, "They were wounded when Korban defended himself against their attack."

"Their attack?" Walter said incredulously.

"Yes. As you know, Korban was...contained." I had locked him up in what essentially amounted to a shed, but I couldn't bring myself to say the words. "There was no way for him to instigate what happened."

"Of course not!" Walter snapped. He climbed to his feet and began pacing across the room. "That's not what I meant. Jason admitted that Rick wanted to kill the tribute due to some ill-conceived notion it would make him Alpha of our pack. Jason went along with him because it was easier than saying no." He paused midstep and looked at me. "I've already talked with my son about his poor decision-making and now I'm here to talk to you."

I had made a lot of poor decisions where Korban was concerned, but the ones Walter knew about were my having demanded a tribute and then imprisoning him. The reason for that was my failure to think through the penalty the interpack council would have given Dirk once they learned about his actions. It was a foolish error on my part, and I wouldn't hide from it.

"I made a mistake," I said. "When I demanded retribution for my father's death, I expected the council to deliver Dirk. I realize now that makes no sense, but—"

"No. That's not why I'm here." He shook his head. "Frankly, Samuel, I had no idea the interpack council could step in and investigate what happened, let alone require a pack to provide a blood tribute. Our entire pack was surprised and extremely impressed with the depth of your knowledge, particularly considering how upset you must have been by...what happened. Expecting to receive the Alpha your father met in the ring mere days earlier makes perfect sense."

I opened my mouth to deny it, to tell him the risk of Dirk being removed from his position had been very real and I should have realized that. But he kept talking.

"Regardless, that isn't why I'm here."

"Oh."

He licked his lips, sighed, and slowly walked toward me. "I'm not here to talk to my Alpha," he said quietly. "I'm here to talk to my friend's son because my friend no longer can."

My chest clenched. I would have loved to have a conversation with my father. Any conversation. Even one where he treated me like a child.

"Samuel."

"Yes."

Walter took in a deep breath. "Jason told me what he saw."

I furrowed my brow in confusion and said, "I don't know what you mean."

"When he came here with Rick. They saw you leaving the workshop." He looked away again and lowered his voice. "They said you weren't dressed, and when they went in, they scented you on the trib—" He froze, and I realized I was growling again. "On Korban Keller," he corrected.

Though Korban had assured me time and again that I hadn't hurt him, that he had wanted us to tie, and that he would have stopped me if he had felt otherwise, I still hated myself for what I'd done to him. Because of that, when I tried to respond, no words came out.

"You have to stop," Walter said. "I know they took your father from you. They took my closest friend from me. They took our Alpha from us. But your father wouldn't have wanted to tarnish your soul with this type of revenge. Torturing a man sexually is unacceptable."

"What? No! I didn't... I mean, I..." I had tied with him, that much I couldn't deny, but I hadn't tortured him. Even when I'd lost control and tied with him in our animal forms, my intent had never been to hurt Korban.

"There's no point in saying it isn't true, Samuel," he said tiredly. "I can smell him on you now. His scent is as strong as yours." He paused and tilted his head to the side. "His scent is as strong as yours," he repeated slowly. "That doesn't make sense." He stepped closer to me. "No matter how much contact a shifter has with someone else, his own scent always remains strongest."

He was talking to himself, processing what his senses were telling him. Walter Clemson was an intelligent man. There was only one possible explanation for my altered scent, and he'd realize exactly what it was on his own, which would be more effective than anything I could say.

"I can smell soap on you too." He had come near enough to touch me, and he did just that, reaching forward and smoothing his hand over my head. "Your hair's damp. That means you just bathed. His scent should have washed off you." His eyebrows furrowed together. "Why hasn't his scent washed off you?"

I stayed still. It wouldn't take him long.

Leaning down, he inhaled deeply. "Wait. His scent isn't on you. It's your scent." He jerked as if I'd hit him. "Your scent is different." He shook his head quickly. "No, that's not right. It's the same, but it's different. And Korban's is there too, below the skin. It's like they're combined, like they're braided together, like—" He gasped and stared at me wide-eyed, realization having set in. "How?"

Tilting one corner of my mouth up in amusement, I raised my eyebrows and gave him a knowing look.

"Not that. I know how, but…" He stumbled over to a chair and collapsed in it. "He's your true mate?"

"Yes," I said proudly. "He is."

"Hey," Korban said as I started walking up the stairs.

I snapped my head up. "Hi." My mind had been on my conversation with Walter and what I needed to do next, so I hadn't noticed him. "How long have you been sitting there?"

"I finished up in the shower pretty soon after you left. Then I called a couple of friends to find out what's going on in Miancarem, but that didn't take long, so"—he smiled softly—"a while."

The living room was immediately adjacent to the open area at the bottom of the stairs, and rather than a doorway, it had a large arched opening. With the way sound traveled, a shifter standing— or in Korban's case, sitting—on the stairs would have been able to make out most of my conversation with Walter.

"How much did you hear?" I asked.

"A lot." He scooted over to the side and opened his arms. "C'mere."

I rushed up the stairs, sat down, and hugged him tightly. "I made so many mistakes."

"You didn't torture me," he said. "You didn't hurt me. I already told you that. Your pack member was wrong."

Though I doubted I'd ever come to terms with the circumstances surrounding our first mating, I knew Korban harbored no bad feelings over it. But it was only one of my mistakes.

"Not only that," I said, burrowing closer to him, surrounding myself in his scent and heat. "I demanded retribution without thinking through all the possible outcomes. Now Miancarem has an issue with its leadership and my pack sees you as nothing more than a tribute. I should have realized that would happen. I should have recognized who you were to me much sooner. I should have admitted to my father that I'd never tied and that was the reason I had trouble shifting into my human form. I should—"

"Whoa, slow down," Korban said. "My brain and my ears need a minute to catch up." He combed his fingers through my hair and kissed my head. "How long had you been having trouble shifting?"

"A few years."

"Me too. Except for me, it was harder to get into my wolf form."

"Really?" I leaned back and processed that statement. "I wonder why. You're male, and male wolves need to tie to hold on to their human halves, not to release their wolves. Plus, your wolf was already free."

Korban sighed. "I've said it before and I'll say it again—just because we've been told we have to live a certain way in order to be whole doesn't mean it's true. Maybe my spirit is more connected to my human half and yours is more connected to your wolf." He shrugged. "It makes sense, right? Your wolf has always been very strong. Even when you were young."

For many years, I had prided myself on that strength, but when my shifting issues intensified and I had to fight that part of my nature to keep it contained, I had started resenting it.

"Asking ourselves why is pointless," Korban said. He held on to the sides of my head and tipped it back until our eyes met. "I know you're a thinker, Samuel, but there might not be a puzzle here to solve. We're true mates. We fit together on a fundamental level. Maybe it's as simple as that."

Considering that viewpoint, I leaned against the railing. "Have you ever studied Greek mythology?"

He shook his head.

"They created really elaborate stories to explain things they didn't have the tools to understand. Having reasons for things is comforting because the alternative is being at the mercy of the unknown. You're saying the same thing."

"I am?"

"Uh-huh. You said pack lore isn't fact. It's a collection of stories our ancestors wrote to explain the unexplainable."

He arched his eyebrows and chuckled. "I'm pretty sure all I said was I want to be with you and that's good enough for me, but, okay. Your thing sounds good too." He nodded. "We can go with that."

"You're teasing me." I bumped my shoulder against his.

"Uh-huh," he said and then bumped me back. "And you're letting me."

I took a deep breath and let it out slowly. "It feels nice."

He reached for my hand, tangled our fingers together, and leaned his head against my shoulder. "It sure does."

After a few minutes of comfortable silence, I said, "You talked with someone about your uncle?"

"Uh-huh. Yoram and his dad."

"What'd they say?"

"Not much. Basically, Dennis stepped in as Alpha when the interpack council said my father couldn't take the position back, even if he recovers."

"How is he?" I asked, not sure what I wanted to hear as the answer. He was my mate's father, so wishing him death was wrong. But I wanted it anyway.

"I didn't ask," Korban said. "I don't care."

A better person would have addressed that response and tried to help him heal the rift with his family. I did neither.

"What do you mean your uncle stepped in as Alpha? He can't just step in."

"He can't?" Korban sat up straight and twisted to the side so we were facing each other.

"No. Only a presumptive Alpha rises to the position automatically."

"But he's my father's only relative now."

As the years passed, people followed the basic rules as they'd seen their parents follow them, but surprisingly, they rarely took the time to actually read the laws that governed our kind.

"That doesn't matter," I explained. "As Alpha, your father can identify the shifter who will one day follow him, which is almost always the Alpha's son. Unless there's another shifter in the pack who is obviously stronger, that identification is enough and the person is considered the presumptive Alpha. That means the Alpha trains him, teaches him, and prepares him to one day lead the pack."

"Right." Korban nodded. "That was me. But I can't be Alpha. The council removed me from the position. Doesn't that leave my uncle to take over?"

"No. He wasn't the presumptive Alpha and he didn't earn a claim to lead the pack. Being a relative of the Alpha isn't relevant."

"Where does that leave the pack?" Korban wrinkled his brow. "They need an Alpha."

"Technically, they have an Alpha."

Korban considered my words. "My father? But I thought because of what he did—"

"Not your father." I met his gaze. "You."

"The interpack council removed me from the position," he argued.

"No," I said vehemently. "They had no cause to remove you as Alpha. That's part of what I should have realized all along. Miancarem took our Alpha in violation of pack rules. That meant under the old laws, we were entitled to demand equivalent retribution—we were entitled to demand an Alpha. But Dirk no longer held the honor because of what he did, so the interpack council delivered you." I waited for a few seconds, letting what I'd said sink in. "They gave us an Alpha, Korban. The tribute was valid because of who you are to the Miancarem pack. You're their Alpha."

He didn't make a sound, didn't take a breath. "I don't want it," he said eventually. "My place is by your side, but..."

We'd make it work. I was Korban's mate. That came first, and whatever else happened, we'd deal with it.

"You said the current Alpha identifies a presumptive Alpha and that person takes over when the Alpha steps down?" Korban said.

"Yes."

"Yoram said he was going to challenge Dennis. He won't stand by and let a weaker man lead the pack, especially because my uncle has all the same faults as my father and none of the power. Yoram's family is well established, so a lot of pack members will be pleased if he unseats Dennis. But those who are loyal to my family line will be angry." He rubbed his palms over his eyes. "It's a mess. But if an Alpha can appoint the presumptive Alpha, and I'm the Alpha—"

"You want to take your rightful place in your pack only to turn around and hand it over to your friend?" I said, suddenly understanding what he was telling me.

He nodded. "Can I do that?"

I thought about it carefully, not wanting to miss an angle and make another mistake.

"Yes, but if there's as much unrest in the pack as you've been told, you're taking a risk of being challenged in the ring."

"What do you mean?"

"Well." I considered all the facts I knew. "An Alpha can be challenged in the ring, as you know. If you claim your place, the shifters who are opposed to the change in leadership might immediately challenge you."

"No. It's not me they're angry with, and even if they were, Yoram would never let them challenge me. He's a loyal friend and he'll know my plan."

"You're referring to the pack members who want your line to leave."

"Yes. Who were you talking about?"

"Your uncle."

Korban swallowed hard. "You think my uncle will challenge me in a fight to the death?"

"It's possible, Korban." I raised our joined hands to my mouth and kissed the underside of his wrist. "I don't know him, but you suspect him of being involved in poisoning my father. He was willing to take a life in exchange for power. How do you know he won't try to do it again?"

"You're right," he admitted. "But I'm stronger than my uncle." He scoffed. "I'm stronger than my father too, which is one reason he doesn't trust me. Even if Dennis challenges me, he won't stand a chance of winning."

The conversation was uncomfortably familiar. "My father thought the same thing," I whispered.

"Oh, honey." Korban's face fell. "I'm sorry. I should have realized." He pulled me onto his lap and held me close. "I won't make you watch me fight." He kissed my neck. "It wasn't fair of me to even suggest it. Like I said, you're my mate. My loyalty rests with you."

"But your pack—"

"The shifters in Miancarem will have to bring themselves out of this mess," he said, his voice strained and his expression pained. "Yafenack is my pack now."

Though I knew he meant what he said—he'd put me first even if it meant standing by as harm came to the pack he'd been raised to lead—and though I loathed the thought of watching a man I loved step into the ring where my father died, I couldn't let an entire pack suffer because of my worries. An Alpha had to be strong enough to make sacrifices for the good of the pack.

My father had been willing to risk himself to take over Miancarem and save them from a weak leader. My mate was willing to risk himself to save the pack he'd been raised in from breaking apart. I could set aside my fears for the good of the pack.

"If you want to do it, I'll stand by you," I said. "I know you're stronger than Dennis, and the pack needs you."

He brushed my hair off my forehead. "You're sure?"

I nodded. "Yes, but I want to come with you." I hoped he wouldn't be offended. "I know they're your pack, your family, but I don't trust them and I want—"

"You want to protect me." He slid his lips over mine. "That's sweet."

Nobody had ever called me sweet. I might have been offended, but he was kissing me and touching me, so I let it go.

"And of course you can come with me. I'm stronger than my uncle in both forms, so I'll be fine, but having you by my side is always a good thing."

He had strength and youth on his side. But the shifter he might be forced to face in the ring had no honor.

"And unlike last time, I know not to trust anybody," I said. "If he challenges you, I'll monitor anyone in the ring with you and all of the witnesses the entire time."

Nobody would hurt my mate. I'd make sure of it.

"You'll keep me safe?"

If Korban would be forced to step into the ring, it'd be because of a challenge by someone in the Miancarem pack, someone he had grown up alongside of, maybe even someone who shared his blood. And yet it was me he relied on for his safety.

"You can count on me."

"I know," he whispered as he gazed at me warmly and caressed my cheek. "I trust you. I'm yours."

And I was his.

CHAPTER 15

WE SPENT the evening cuddled together on the couch in the family room going over our plan for Korban's return to Miancarem and how he would announce to the pack—and his uncle—that he was their Alpha. I didn't want to risk anything going amiss and endangering my mate, so I allowed no stone to be left unturned in our discussion. Only when I was certain we had considered every possible risk and outcome—and when Korban begged for mercy from what he described as my torturing him by way of conversation—did I allow us to move on.

"We're done?" he asked disbelievingly. "Like done done? No more 'Oh, but what if...' possibilities to dissect?"

"You're teasing me," I grumbled, crossing my arms over my chest.

He scooped me into a hug and lightly bit my neck. "Mostly. But, seriously, do you want to talk about this some more? Because I can if you need to."

"No, I'm good," I assured him. "Honestly."

"Oh, thank God." He let out a deep breath.

I arched my eyebrows.

"It's not that I wasn't interested in the conversation, but, uh, I'm tired and we need to be up early and...do you want a drink?" He got up from the sofa and pointed toward the kitchen. "Or a snack? I'm going to get some water."

Unable to keep a straight face, I laughed. "All right, all right already." I got up and shook my head. "I'm scary overthinker guy. I get it." I leaned over and kissed his cheek. "Go get your water. I'll meet you upstairs."

He winked and then walked into the kitchen as I headed up the stairs. My mother's timing had always been impeccable, and that night was no different. As soon as I walked into the bedroom, my phone rang.

"Hi, Mom."

"Samuel," she sighed in relief. "It's good to hear your voice. How are you doing?" She paused. "The truth, now."

For years I had downplayed the depth of my shifting problem and the anxiety it caused me. She must have realized that, which wasn't surprising considering how bad things had gotten and how observant she was. I was happy to finally ease her worries about me while answering her question honestly.

"I'm good." I stepped out of my shoes and placed them on the rack in the closet. "Really good." My socks were next; I shook them out and dropped them into the laundry basket.

"You sound it. I got a call from Walter Clemson today. Based on your voice, I assume the news he gave me was accurate. You found your true mate?"

As close as Walter had been to my father throughout their lives, it made sense that he had formed a friendship with my mother as well, so I understood why he'd contacted her. After all, it wasn't every day a person heard about a shifter having a true mate. And if the shifter was male and his true mate was too, well, that was even more rare; so rare, in fact, I had gone all of my life without knowing it could happen.

"Yes," I said as I walked to the bed. "You're going to adore him."

It was only after I said the words that I realized I had no idea how much information Walter had given my mother. If she didn't know my mate was male, I should have shared that detail more delicately.

"I've met Korban Keller once or twice. He's delightful and his smile lights up a room," she said, immediately easing my worries. "I knew his mother, you know."

"You did?" I sat down on the edge of the mattress. "How?"

"She was married to the Alpha of a neighboring pack, and I was married to the presumptive Alpha of our pack, so we found ourselves at the same places several times. Korban takes after her in both appearance and disposition. It's a shame she passed so young. She was a joy, and I never understood what she saw in her mate."

"I'm glad to hear that," I said. "Well, not the last part but...you know what I mean."

Chuckling, my mother said, "Yes, I know what you mean." She cleared her throat. "How long have you known he was your true mate?"

Shameful though it was to admit I had missed something so fundamental for so very long, I had promised myself never again to be dishonest as a way to save my pride. Owning up to my mistakes was difficult and humbling, but if I expected honesty from my pack as their leader, I had to show the same strength of character.

"I just realized it. All those years... I didn't know, Mom."

"During my stay here in Etzgadol, I've had the opportunity to talk to their Alpha."

"I spoke with Zev Hassick too," I told her. "He has a male mate."

"Yes, he does, and he told me being raised to believe males could only tie with females made it a fair bit harder for him to recognize his true mate for who he was." She paused. "I wish we'd known it was possible, Samuel. Your father and I would have helped you. A true mate is a blessing. It's the greatest honor a shifter can have. I know that. Your father knew that," she said hoarsely and then cleared her throat. "Being mated to a male wouldn't have diminished the importance of that, not to us."

"That means a lot to me, Mom. Thank you."

"He's already made an impact on you," she said. "I don't remember the last time we had a conversation for this long without you fidgeting like you had ants in your pants and doing everything you could to be done talking."

I laughed at the amusing and admittedly accurate image she painted. "Maybe I'm doing that ant dance now and you don't know because you're on the phone so you can't see me."

"I can tell, Samuel. You're my son and I know you. Besides, the fact that you're joking about an ant dance instead of being confused about what I meant or acting defensive and saying I'm treating you like a child proves I'm right."

As my mother was speaking, Korban walked into the bedroom. Immediately my heart lurched. He was so beautiful he took my breath away.

My mother was right. "He's good for me," I said as I reached my hand out to him.

Beaming happily, he headed over to me and straddled my lap.

"You've always been a good boy," she said. "You work so much and try so hard." Her voice broke. "I'm glad you have someone made just for you. You deserve it."

"I'm not sure about that," I said sincerely. "But I'll do everything I can to earn it." I gazed at Korban and cupped his cheek. "To deserve him."

"Oh, Samuel. I never thought I'd hear you talk that way about anyone," she said, her voice breaking. After pausing for a moment and clearing her throat, she continued. "Now that you're feeling strong and have your mate, I take it you plan to remain Alpha of the Yafenack pack?"

"Yes."

"Good." Her tone changed from soft and shaky to firm and determined. It was her "I mean business" voice. "This has been a nice trip, but it's time for us to come home. Jen and Eddie and I will say our goodbyes and be back in Yafenack in a few days. I'll put together a party to celebrate your mating and introduce Korban to the pack. Nothing formal, maybe a potluck in the backyard. Or a barbeque. I'll figure it out."

There was no stopping my mother when she was in one of her determined moods, not that I wanted to stop her. I liked the idea of welcoming the pack into our home and having them meet my mate.

"Thank you."

"I'll see you soon. It's getting late and I need to turn in for the night," she said. "Give my best to Korban and tell him I'm looking forward to getting to know him."

"I will. Good night, Mom."

"Good night."

Keeping one arm wrapped around Korban so he wouldn't slide off my lap, I reached over to the nightstand and set the phone down.

"How's your mom?" he asked as he combed his fingers through the back of my hair and massaged my nape.

"Good." I lay down flat on my back and he stayed on top of me. "She's excited to get to know you when she comes home."

"I am too. When is she coming back?"

"In a few days. So are my brother and sister."

"That's great."

"Uh-huh." I pushed one hand under his shirt and rubbed his back. "She wants to throw a party so you can meet the pack."

"I love parties." He grinned. "That sounds like fun."

I traced his lips with my finger and wondered how I ever found that open joy suspicious. "You used to smile at me like this when we were kids," I said, thinking out loud.

He swiped his tongue out and took my finger into his mouth, sucking until I was breathless before he released me. "And you thought I was a dangerous element."

"Not dangerous, but—" I drew in a deep breath. "Something seemed different or strange. It confused me and I didn't like that."

"I'm sure you didn't." He kissed my palm and then licked it. "You like order and control and rules that fit in neat boxes. I bet you had yourself all twisted up in knots when you realized I was your true mate."

"But I didn't know."

With his forearms planted on the mattress to hold him up, Korban's face was right above mine. He gazed into my eyes. "You knew." He rubbed our noses together. "Deep down in your gut, you knew. But it didn't fit in your world order, so your brain kept it out."

He could have been right, but that didn't change how hard it must have been for him to be ignored by his mate. "Thanks for being patient with me," I whispered as I pushed his hair off his face.

"You needed time." He leaned forward and slid his lips over mine. "I'll always give you what you need."

Of that I had no doubt. "Korban?" I rasped as I dug my fingers into his lower back and massaged the tight muscles.

"Yeah?" He moaned and arched his back, pushing against my fingers. "Mmm, that feels good."

"I want you." I bucked my hips, nudging my erection against him.

"Take me." He rolled his groin over mine. "I'm yours." He lowered his mouth to mine. "Always yours."

From the start, the kiss was intense. Korban bit my lip and tugged, tilted his head, and then pushed his tongue into my mouth.

"Ungh," I moaned, and I gripped his waist, holding on tightly while he plundered my mouth and ground his hard dick against my belly.

"How do you want me, honey?" he asked.

"I want." I gulped. "Do you think you can trust me to...to... I know before I was rough and out of control, but I want to... I want to..."

"You want to make love to me?"

He spoke the words so easily, so sincerely.

"Yes," I said hoarsely. I moved my hands down his back and squeezed his muscular globes. "I want that so much. But we don't have to if you're scared because of what I did."

"I'm not scared of you, Samuel. I have never been scared of you." He rose to his knees and stripped off his shirt. "The first couple of times we tied were intense, but not bad." He unbuttoned his jeans, pushed them and his briefs down his thighs, and then rolled onto his back and wiggled out of them, leaving himself completely nude. "Though I have to admit, I'm looking forward to experiencing what you can do in this form."

Watching him undress had me throbbing in my pants. Every part of him aroused me—his kind face, his lean chest, his thick dick, his muscular thighs.

"Where do you want me?" he asked.

Too turned on to speak, all I could do was devour him with my eyes.

"Like this?" He turned around and dropped to all fours, giving me a close view of his firm backside.

"Oh God," I gasped and reached for myself, rubbing my palm down my dick and over my balls.

"Do I turn you on?" he asked playfully as he looked at me over his shoulder. He wagged his ass from side to side. "Come and get me."

Despite being hard to the point of madness, I laughed. "You're fun," I told him as I started undressing.

"No. I'm..." He furrowed his brow. "I'm hot. I'm sexy. I'm any other word that means you want me. I'm not fun. Fun isn't going to get me laid."

"I do want you." I arched my back and shoved my pants and briefs down. "And being fun will absolutely get you laid."

With his gaze locked on my erect cock, Korban licked his lips. "Yeah, okay, I'm fun." He turned back around so he was facing forward, propped his forearms on the bed, and tilted his ass up. "Come on. I want to feel you inside."

I grabbed the lotion from where we'd left it on the nightstand and then kneeled behind him.

"You are so beautiful," I said as I cupped both sides of his butt and ran my thumbs up and down his crease. "All of you, inside and out." I sighed. "Beautiful."

Korban widened his stance, spreading himself open and showing me the entrance to the tight channel where I wanted to bury myself. When I gently moved my finger over the sensitive skin, he trembled.

There were so many things I wanted to do all at once—kiss his plump lips, suck his perfect dick, slide into his hot body, and touch every inch of his smooth skin. Only the knowledge I'd have my entire life to devote to those tasks, to learn all the ways I could make him moan with pleasure and sigh in satisfaction, kept me from losing my mind. Holding his cheeks apart, I dipped forward and flicked my tongue over his pucker.

"Oh!" he cried out. "Oh God, honey, yes." He lowered his face and shoulders to the mattress and raised his ass higher, exposing himself more. "Touch me."

The trust he put in me was humbling and exciting. With as turned on as I was, I knew I had to get inside him soon, but first I wanted to taste more. Flattening my tongue, I licked up and down his crease before returning my attention to his rosebud. I curled my tongue and pushed it inside his hole, moving in and out as he gasped and whimpered in pleasure. When Korban tightened his muscle around my tongue and pushed his backside against my face, I almost came.

"I need to be inside you," I said as I scrambled up to a kneeling position.

"Want you," he responded, his voice rough with arousal.

With my hands shaking, I picked up the lotion, poured some onto my fingers, and pushed it into his body.

"Yes," he hissed.

I slicked my cock, curled my chest over his back, and planted one hand on the bed while I held my dick against his pucker with the other. "Love you," I whispered as I slowly slid inside silky heat. When I was all the way in and my balls made contact with his skin, I covered his hands with mine, curled our fingers together, and then kissed his nape. "Love you so much."

He twisted his head back, looked into my eyes, and licked my lips. "I love you too, Samuel."

A wave of intense emotion and overpowering affection rolled over me, bringing tears to my eyes. I squeezed his hands and, with my gaze locked on his, slowly pulled out, groaning at the glide of skin against skin. When only my crown remained inside his body, I paused and then thrust forward hard.

"Ah!" Korban yelled. "Yes. Like that." He curled his neck down and tilted his hips up. "I want it like that."

We wanted the same thing. With his hands firmly in my grip and my body blanketing his, I held on to him and started pumping my dick in and out of his tight hole, speeding up my pace with every thrust. Korban gasped and moaned, moving in concert with me, and when I changed the angle of penetration and slid my cockhead against his gland, he shouted.

"Samuel!" He arched his back. "Oh God, fuck me." Straightening his arms, he braced himself and started pushing back with fury. "Fuck me. Fuck me."

Any control I had left vanished, and I bit his shoulder, not piercing the skin, but just needing another way to hold on, to keep him close. Our balls slapped together as I pounded into him with every ounce of strength I possessed.

"A little more, just a little more," Korban mumbled.

A little would never be enough, not when our connection burned so hot, but it was all I could give in that moment because my orgasm came barreling at me. Shoving into his channel as deep as I could, I felt my mating knot grow and lock us together just as I opened my mouth and then bit down, using my sharp canines to dig into the spot where I had already marked him as my mate. My seed pulsed from me in powerful bursts, filling his body.

"Samuel!" he cried out as his hole tightened around me and he came.

I lapped at his skin, nuzzled his neck, and rubbed my thumbs over the sides of his hands, trying to gentle us both as our burning lungs and racing hearts slowed.

"Wow," he said breathlessly after a couple of minutes. "I don't know what to say about that." He sucked in more air. "Wow."

"Wow is good, right?"

"Uh-huh." He turned his head to the side and kissed my shoulder. "So good."

"I love making you feel good." I wrapped my arm around his waist and held him against me as I rolled us onto our sides. Then I curled myself around him and slid my other arm under his head as a pillow. "And I love making you scream," I whispered and then kissed his nape. "It turns me on so much." I was still tied to him, so I rolled my hips, reminding him that I was there, deep inside his body.

"You're amazing at that." He sighed contentedly. "Seriously amazing. Like 'I'll be begging for it again and again on a daily basis' amazing, but"—he turned his head and landed his sparkling gaze on mine—"we have to move out of this house, because I won't be able to look your mom in the face if she hears the way you make me scream."

CHAPTER 16

As it turned out, Korban's begging was more frequent than he predicted. Although begging might not be the right description because he didn't need to use words. He simply took me in hand and stroked me until I woke up, then he shoved his tongue in my mouth and climbed onto my erection, riding us both into sweaty, sticky oblivion. Twice.

"Are you awake?" I whispered into his ear the next morning as I caressed his flank.

We were chest to chest. Our legs were tangled together, he had his arm curled around my waist, and I had mine wrapped around his back.

"Uh-huh. You want to go again?" he said, slurring his words because he wasn't fully awake. "We can go again."

Chuckling, I squeezed his hip. "Want? Definitely. But as much as I wish I could stay here locked away with you all day, I can't. And neither can you. The packs need us."

"Nuh-uh." He shook his head and buried his face under my chin. "Don't wanna."

It was hard not to laugh at his antics. "Quit acting like a child. You're an Alpha."

"I'm tired. You fucked me into the mattress twice last night."

"Three times."

He raised his head and blinked his eyes open. "Oh yeah." A slow smile spread across his face. "That third time was really something. How'd you think of that position?"

Heat flowed up my neck and cheeks. "I wasn't, uh, thinking, really. I was just moving and, um...you liked it?"

I had rolled Korban onto his right side, pushed his left leg up to his chest, and then bent over him and pounded into his hole.

"I came without touching my dick and shot so hard I hit my chin. And that was the third time that night. So, yeah." He nodded. "I liked it." He paused, tilted his head to the side, and looked at me appraisingly. "Are you blushing?"

"No, I...uh, maybe." I ducked my head.

"You are! You're blushing. You're the one who did the act, but hearing me say the words has you burning up." He rolled me onto my back and peppered my face with kisses. "That's very cute and it makes me want to do all sorts of really dirty things to see if those embarrass you too."

"Okay, let's get ahold of ourselves here. We have a plan for today, and if we don't get out of bed, we'll never..." His words finally registered. "What kinds of dirty things?" I shook the thought away, trying to focus. "Never mind. We need to get out of bed, shower, eat, and then go to Miancarem."

"Fine," he sighed dramatically and then climbed off me. "You're a spoilsport." He slid off the bed. "But don't worry. I'll demonstrate some of those dirty things when we get home tonight."

He sauntered into the bathroom, shaking his firm butt, and I focused on not swallowing my tongue.

"Samuel?" Korban called out right as the shower started running. "I think we can do one of those dirty things in here and keep it relatively clean. Are you coming?"

I did. And so did he. And we both screamed.

He was right. We needed to find a place of our own. Living with my mother and siblings was absolutely not an option.

"You're alive," Dennis Keller said when he opened his front door and laid eyes on Korban. "Why are you still alive?"

It wasn't the most welcoming of welcomes.

"Hi, Dennis," Korban said. "I'm not sure how to answer that question. I feel like maybe I should respond with that quote from that guy about his death reports being exaggerated."

"Mark Twain," I whispered.

"What?" Korban turned to me.

"The quote you're talking about. 'Reports of my death have been greatly exaggerated.' That was Mark Twain. But did you know those weren't his exact words?" I said excitedly. "What he actually said was—"

"Who is he?" Dennis said, interrupting me.

Annoyed, I stepped closer to him and looked him the eyes. He paled, telling me he realized exactly who I was.

"Why are you here?" He gulped and darted his gaze back and forth between Korban and me. "What's going on?"

"Are we going to have this conversation on your front porch?" Korban asked.

Instead of inviting us inside, his uncle reached behind him for the doorknob and pulled the half-open door closed. "Out here is fine," he said shakily.

I had never considered myself skilled at reading body language or understanding people's emotions, but I was pretty sure Dennis was nervous. My initial thought was that he knew his assertion about becoming Alpha of Miancarem simply by virtue of being Dirk Keller's relative was false. I was quickly disabused of that notion.

"Okay, then I'll cut to the chase," Korban said. "As you noticed, I'm not dead, which means I'm still Alpha of this pack. I heard there may be some confusion about that, so I wanted to let you know. I'm calling a pack meeting for tomorrow evening and I'll fill everyone in on my plans."

"You can't be Alpha," Dennis said. "The interpack council took you away."

"The council offered our pack's Alpha—that's me"—he gestured to himself with his thumb—"to the Yafenack pack as a blood tribute in compensation for my father's violations. They chose not to kill me." He pulled his shoulders back and stood straight and proud. "So I'm still Alpha."

"But this isn't how it's supposed to work. Dirk said they'd deliver your body and then..." His eyes widened and he slammed his mouth shut.

"My father said a lot of things. None of them matter now."

"He can't take over our pack that way!" Dennis screeched and pointed at me.

It was really inappropriate for any sort of leader to take that hysterical tone. Plus, it wasn't the least bit effective as far as intimidation tactics went. I crossed my arms over my chest and stared at him without saying a word.

"He can't." Backing up a step, he bumped into his doorjamb and said, "You think you can fool me, Korban, but you can't. I know what's going on. You traded your life for this...this...ruse."

"I have no idea what you're talking about," Korban said in annoyance. "I didn't say Samuel was taking over the pack. I said I'm still Alpha."

Dennis narrowed his eyes suspiciously. "Then why is he here?"

Shaking his head, Korban sighed in frustration. "Samuel is with me because he's my true mate and he didn't like the idea of me coming here unprotected after what my father and you did to his dad."

"Your true mate?" Dennis spat. "That's impossible and disgusting! He can't be—"

"He can and he is," Korban snapped.

I reached out to him. Korban looked down and then laid his palm on mine. His shoulders relaxed and the tension left his face. Taking in a deep breath, he turned back to his uncle.

"Make whatever telephone calls you want to make to confirm how the rules work," Korban said. "The pack meeting will be in the community center tomorrow evening at six. Come or don't come. Either way, I'm Alpha."

He started down the front walk, and I stayed beside him, still holding his hand. When we got to the car, I squeezed it and then stepped around to the passenger side. Korban knew who we were going to visit in Miancarem, so he was driving.

"Your relationship with your family is a little, um, tense," I said once we were in the car and out of his uncle's hearing range.

Sighing, he dragged his fingers through his hair and then slumped against the seat. "My uncle is pretty much a puppet for my father, always has been. Even though nobody admitted it, I've always suspected that was the reason my aunt left him."

"They're divorced?" I asked in surprise. Though some shifter marriages ended, it wasn't a common occurrence.

"Yup." Korban nodded. "My aunt and my mother were really close, so I spent a lot of time at her house. She had two daughters, and the three of us played together all the time. I was too young to understand what was going on between the adults, but I remember my aunt and my father argued a lot. Nobody talked back to my father, which is why I noticed it."

He paused and looked out at the woods, his brow wrinkled in concentration. "Then, right around the time my mom died, my aunt came to my school. I was in the playground out front, and she walked up, gave me a hug, and told me she loved me and not to worry because we'd see each other soon." He closed his eyes. "I never saw her or my cousins again."

I reached across the console and squeezed his arm. "I'm sorry. It must have been really hard for you to lose them both so close together, and your cousins too."

"I was pretty young, so I don't remember a lot of it, but, yeah. It sucked." He sighed. "At first, my father spent a lot of time with me, letting me see what it was like to be Alpha because it'd be my job one day." He shrugged. "It was fine, but the older I got, the clearer it became we didn't agree on much, and then after I met you..." He lifted my hand to his mouth and kissed it. "My father has been at odds with the Smiths my entire life because he agreed with my great-grandfather that Yoram's gay uncle couldn't be in the pack. It was hard enough when I chose Yoram for a friend and wouldn't stop hanging around with him, but once I realized I had a male true mate—" He chuckled and shook his head. "No way could I tell my father the truth about me. You saw how my uncle was just now. My father would have been worse. I used to hope that maybe, over time, I could work on him and get him to change his mind about Yoram's uncle and then he'd see it was fine by the time I was old enough to mate. Instead all that happened is we grew further and further apart and I cared less and less."

My memory of Korban was of a happy, carefree boy who everyone loved. I'd had no idea he had lost so much as a child and had been living under a mountain of pressure the entire time.

"I wish I had been there for you," I said as I twisted sideways and cupped his cheek.

"You were." He turned his head into my palm and licked it. "Those few times we saw each other and played together were what got me through day after day." He smiled, the expression genuine and relaxed. "I know you keep beating yourself up about not realizing I was your mate, and believe me, I remember how prickly you were in those days." He combed his fingers through my hair. "But we had a lot of fun together back then, and I knew someday I'd get to have that all the time."

He clasped the back of my head and tugged me forward for a kiss. "And now someday is here and you're mine." He nipped my chin and then faced forward and turned on the car. "Let's get going before my uncle and my father pull those curtains off the rods."

Jerking my gaze toward Dennis's house, I said, "Your father was there?"

"I'm pretty sure he was, yeah."

"How do you know? His scent was all around, but that doesn't mean he was there today. It could be that he's spent a lot of time there."

"It wasn't because of his scent," Korban said as he pulled away from the curb. "Like you said, my father is there so much it's impossible to know from the scent outside if he's inside. But from the way my uncle was acting all twitchy and nervous, I'd bet a pretty penny my father was in the house listening to our entire conversation or waiting for Dennis to come report every word."

After giving myself a moment to feel proud that I'd been right about Dennis acting nervous, I refocused on the conversation.

"Do you think that means your father isn't as injured as everyone was led to believe?"

"Huh." Korban flicked his gaze toward me and then back to the road. "I hadn't thought of that. It isn't like my father to admit to any sort of weakness, though, so I don't know why he'd pretend to be ill."

"Hmm." I considered what would lead a proud-to-the-point-of-arrogant man who relished power more than anything else to fake being powerless. "Your uncle mentioned something about expecting your body to be delivered. He said your father told him that's what would happen."

"Right."

"He also said you were pretending to be my mate in exchange for your life."

Korban scoffed. "He's a fool if he thinks you'd do something like that. Anyone who knows anything about you knows you're honorable and by the book. Besides, what would be the point?"

My heart warmed at my mate's praise. Of all the reasons his uncle's accusation made no sense, he focused on my good character as the main point. I gazed at Korban's handsome profile—his defined cheekbones, straight nose, freckle-smattered ivory skin, and plump lips. The man looked like an angel, all innocence and light. With what I'd just learned about his family, his upbringing, and his struggles, I was in awe of his ability to maintain that sweetness and joy. He was remarkable.

"Korban?" I said hoarsely, my throat thick with emotion.

"Uh-huh."

"I love you."

Jerking his gaze toward me, he opened his mouth in surprise and then turned back to the road and smiled. "I love you too. And wow."

"Wow?"

"Samuel Goodwin just told me he loved me in broad daylight with his clothes on and no orgasm in sight." He waggled his eyebrows. "Wow."

Had I only shared my feelings for him when we'd been in bed? I would do better.

When I was younger and my mother had forced me to sit and listen to her advice about courting girls, there had been firm suggestions about using words and giving praise. I had done my best to be patient while she spoke without actually listening to anything she said because I had been so uncomfortable, but maybe if I focused, I could recall some of it. If not, I was certain she'd be willing to tell me if I asked again. It'd be shameful to admit I didn't know how to treat my mate, but the alternative was not giving him everything he deserved, and that was unacceptable.

"Stop doing that thing where you beat yourself up for no reason," he said, reaching over to rub my arm with one hand, keeping the other on the wheel. "We've known each other most of our lives, but our mating is very new and we've spent almost all our time together with our pants off. So, really, outside of this little excursion, you'd be hard-pressed to find more than a few combined minutes when we weren't about to get off, getting off, or recovering from having gotten off."

I had no idea how to react to his crude language. Or why it had my cock filling.

"You're blushing right now, aren't you?" he said.

And now my mate was teasing me again. If I didn't enjoy it so much, I'd definitely put a stop to it. "Keep your eyes on the road," I grumbled.

Throwing his head back, he laughed. "Okay, okay. Just tell me this."

His tone alone was enough to put me on guard. I knew he was up to no good.

"Are your cheeks the only place blood is flowing, or is it also moving south?"

"We're in the car," I pointed out sharply.

"Uh-huh."

"And we're about to visit your friend and his family to talk about very serious matters."

After seemingly thinking that over for a few seconds, he said, "Good point. Getting you all hot and bothered when I can't do anything about it sucks. I'll cool it for now and then talk dirty again when we're heading home. That way the only sucking will be the good kind."

There was absolutely no way for me to keep the image of his lips wrapped around my cock out of my head. None. My dick went from semihard to ready to go.

"Korban," I groaned.

"Okay, I'll stop!" He chuckled a bit more and then cleared his throat. "So what were we talking about?"

I had no idea. My attention was well and truly thrown.

"Oh, right. My uncle's weird thing about you taking over the Miancarem pack by pretending to be my mate. It makes no sense. Plus, he has to know that if he's actually Alpha and you want to take the pack, all you have to do is challenge him. He won't stand a chance against you in human form, and your wolf will eviscerate him in seconds."

My mate thought I was strong. I puffed up with pride. Truly, I had never had so much trouble focusing.

"Actually, I can't challenge him," I said. "Even if he was Alpha of Miancarem, I wouldn't be able to do it. I had my chance in the ring with your father and I got disqualified, which is the same thing as losing. The rules prohibit a shifter from trying to lead a pack through a challenge more than once."

"They do?"

The first thing I'd do as Alpha would be talk with the schoolteachers. We had to implement studies about pack rules. Though some of our pack lore had turned out to be false and the rules were considered antiquated, they were still enforced, and it wasn't safe for shifters to grow up with no knowledge of them.

"Yes. Otherwise, a shifter who wants to be Alpha would keep calling for a challenge over and over again," I explained.

"But fights in the ring are usually to the death."

"They are unless someone admits defeat and surrenders. If a shifter knows he can come back and try again another day, then he might do exactly that. Call a challenge, fight until he sees he's losing, then surrender, and start the whole thing over again when he's healed." I shook my head. "That would keep the Alpha in a constant state of distraction and injury, which endangers the pack. So the rules don't let it happen. A shifter gets one bite at the apple. If he loses a challenge, he can no longer seek to unseat the Alpha of that pack."

"Oh." Korban bit his lip.

I wanted to lick it and suck it into my mouth.

"You can't fight to be Alpha of Miancarem, so my uncle thinks you're trying to find some other weird way to do it even though you never asked for it to begin with?"

"It's a possibility. Your father knows he can't challenge anyone for the position because of what he did. So his only way to maintain control of the pack is to do exactly what your uncle accused me of doing—put someone else in place as Alpha and then run the pack through him."

"That's manipulative and self-serving, which sounds just like my father."

"Plus, it could explain why he's keeping a low profile right now. He knows you're Alpha so long as you're alive."

Just thinking about what Dirk was doing made me simultaneously ill and enraged, so I couldn't bring myself to articulate the rest of my theory. Korban had no such compunction.

"So, dear old Dad is sitting around waiting for my dead body to be delivered, and then he'll go back to business as usual, running the pack, except my uncle will be in place as a surrogate Alpha."

Hearing the words out loud was even worse than thinking them. I thought nothing could be more horrible than losing my father right before my eyes, but I was wrong. My father had loved me, cared for me, and wanted what was best for me every moment of my life. Korban's father had mistreated him for years and now wanted him dead. I wished I had killed him in that ring.

"It's just a guess," I said. "Maybe I'm wrong." But I doubted it. My logic was solid; it accounted for all the facts we knew; it fit.

"You're right and we both know it." He pulled up in front of a yellow house, turned off the car, and looked at me. "You're brilliant, Samuel. Completely brilliant. You know every detail of every rule and you can make sense of things that make no sense. I admire you so much." He dipped his chin and picked at his jeans. "I hope you don't regret having me for a mate. I don't know as much as you. My wolf isn't as strong. And my brain doesn't..." He bit his lip. "I'm not as smart."

"You are everything I could ever want or hope to have." I climbed to my knees, leaned over, and grasped both sides of his head, forcing him to meet my gaze. "You're sensitive and kind, optimistic and resilient, funny and charismatic." He was everything I wasn't. "You're the other half of me."

His eyes wet, Korban nodded and clutched my wrists. "Yes." He rubbed our noses together. "My true mate," he whispered, and he leaned his forehead against mine. "My perfect mate."

CHAPTER 17

"THIS IS getting ridiculous," I said as I flopped onto my back and sucked air into my burning lungs.

"What?" Korban sounded just as breathless.

"I don't think it's normal for people to, uh"—I tried to think of the right words—"spend this much time in bed."

"I know." He flung both arms out to his sides, landing one hand on my sweaty thigh. Then he skated it up to my groin and cupped my balls. "I feel sorry for them."

I coughed out a laugh.

"What?"

"Nothing." I shook my head. "What do you want to do now?"

"What do you mean?" he asked.

"I don't know." I shrugged. "I just thought we could do something new."

"Something new?"

"Yes." Not that what we'd been doing wasn't good. It had been really good. But I was starting to get dehydrated.

"Umm, I saw this movie where one guy was leaning against the wall and the other guy was doing a handstand, so they were, like, face to dick and they sucked each other off. Like a standing-up sixty-nine." He rolled onto his side, propped his elbow on the bed, and rested his head on his hand. "We could do that."

That was not at all what I meant. I had been thinking cards or a movie. "I don't think that's—"

"No? Okay. I have another one," he said excitedly, making me wonder how he had any energy left after the long day we'd had—we'd seen his uncle and other pack members, gone grocery shopping, and then spent the previous hour mauling each other. "In another movie, one guy was bent in half with his shoulders on the floor and his ankles practically pinned to his ears. Then the other guy was squatting over him and pushing his dick inside his hole." He looked at me expectantly. "That's an option too."

"Please tell me you're joking around," I said, trying to remove the images he was painting from my mind.

"That one's not good either? No worries, I'm sure I can think of more." He pressed his lips together and wrinkled his brow. "I know. Do you have a weight bench, duct tape, and an ice bucket?"

I absolutely did not want to let him finish that description.

"I think the ways we've been doing it are perfect. Plus, they involve a bed, which is more comfortable than the floor, and they require considerably less acrobatics and no props."

"Then why did you ask for ideas of what to do?"

"I wasn't asking for ideas of how to have sex!"

"Oh, thank God." He sighed in relief. "I was worried one of us would sprain something. Plus, I'm all out of suggestions."

My stomach picked that moment to growl. "I think that's for the best." I turned onto my side and caressed his hip. "Besides, my stomach just piped in with a great suggestion about what we should do." I kissed his chin and then sat up. "We need to make dinner so we can replenish all the calories we burned."

"Good call. Plus, we'll need to stock up on more calories so we can burn them tonight." He waggled his eyebrows. "Have I mentioned how much I love your sex drive?"

"Remember you said that when our dicks are falling off from overuse," I said as I got out of bed.

He knee-walked on the bed over to me, cupped my balls and flaccid dick, and nuzzled my neck. "It won't fall off. Worst thing that can happen is a little chafing."

"Hmm." I pressed my lips together and pretended to think that over. "Chafing?"

"Yup." He dipped his head. "And I'll kiss it and make it better." His blue eyes twinkled. "See? Totally worth it."

I snorted in amusement. "I agree, but there is no way I'm getting it up again right now. My stomach won't stop growling, and these hunger pangs are like ice picks stabbing into my gut, so we need to put all potentially genital-injuring activities aside until after dinner."

He squeezed my package. "Or I can kiss it now."

Moaning, I stepped away before he proved me and medical science wrong by making me hard yet again. "We have to eat. You take a shower first and I'll work on making dinner. Then when you're done, we can switch."

He pouted, which was adorable and made me want to kiss him. The man was like an addiction.

"Or we can shower together and then work on dinner," he said.

"If I get under that water with you, the shower will take ten times as long and we'll both make headway on that chafing goal."

"You're right," he said as he got out of bed and walked over to me. I opened my arms, and he stepped into a hug, resting his head on my shoulder. "We should divide and conquer. That's smarter."

I dropped my hands to his backside and kneaded his firm muscles. "What should we make for dinner?"

He traced invisible lines on my back. "How about lasagna? We picked up everything we need for that and a salad at the store."

"I'm not a very skilled cook," I admitted. "But I'm good at following instructions. They were on the box, right?"

"Uh-huh," he said. "I'm not bad in the kitchen. Want me to start the lasagna and you take first shower?"

"No." I shook my head. "I need to learn. That way you won't get stuck doing all the cooking for the rest of our lives."

He lifted his head and smiled at me. "I like the sound of that."

I knew he wasn't talking about the cooking part. "Me too."

It wasn't the neatest-looking lasagna I'd ever seen, but between the cheese, beef, tomato sauce, and pasta, it was sure to taste pretty good. And I had managed to assemble it myself. I had just slid it into the oven when Korban walked into the kitchen wearing a pair of well-fitting black jeans and nothing else.

One of our stops in Miancarem had been to his place. We had packed up his things and brought them home with us. Because we knew we'd be moving out of my family home, there was no point in opening the boxes, so we left them stacked in a corner of the garage. But we brought in a suitcase full of clothes so Korban could wear his own things.

"How was the shower?" I asked as I dragged my gaze up and down his body. Gorgeous. My mate was gorgeous.

"Lonely, but good," he said with a wink. He walked up and leaned against me, the gesture affectionate and familiar. "Tell me where you are with dinner, and I'll have it ready by the time you're done."

"The lasagna is in the oven. I put the timer on. I know you said something about a salad, but there weren't instructions and I wasn't sure where to start."

"I'll take care of it." He kissed my cheek. "Next time, we'll do this together and I can share some tips. It'll be fun."

Though I'd never before had an interest in cooking, I liked the idea of creating something together. "That sounds good. I'll clean up in here and then go shower."

"Don't worry about the cleanup. I'll do the dishes while you're upstairs."

"Are you sure? I don't want to leave you with a mess."

"Mess? What mess?" He looked around the kitchen. "This place is practically spotless. Let me guess, you're one of those clean-while-you-go types, aren't you?"

"I like order. When things aren't where they're supposed to be, I can't focus on anything else," I explained, hoping that wouldn't make me sound as rigid as I probably was. I didn't want Korban to be worried about living with me.

"Oh, good," he said. "You can help me stay organized. I'm sick of never being able to find what I'm looking for."

Relieved, I nuzzled his throat. "I can do that."

"Mmm, feels good," he whispered, tipping his head back to give me more room.

I lapped my tongue over the mating mark on his shoulder and rubbed my thumbs over his nipples. Immediately, he grasped my shoulders and bucked.

"Love how sensitive these are," I said. "Makes me want to suck on them."

He whimpered, letting me know he approved of my idea. "You need to go shower before I start begging you to do that right now," he said.

I wove my fingers through his hair, held his head still, and plundered his mouth, kissing and licking until he was whimpering and using my shoulders to stay upright. Then I pulled away, nipped his lower lip, and said, "Be right back," before forcing myself to walk out of the kitchen.

I got clean sheets from the linen closet, changed the bed, and started the washing machine. Then I took Korban's clothes out of his suitcase and put them away in the closet. Satisfied that the space would look welcoming to him, I got undressed and stepped into the shower.

Not one to dawdle, I ran through the basics—soap, shampoo, shave—then I turned off the water. I was standing on the bathmat, rubbing a towel over my hair, when my skin suddenly prickled and every nerve went on high alert.

"Korban?" I said, even though I knew he wouldn't be able to hear me all the way down in the kitchen.

For a second there was nothing, and then he was there, in my head—sad, scared, hurt, and calling for me. It was just one word, my name: Samuel. But it made me shift into my wolf so quickly that four paws hit the floor before the towel I'd been holding.

Within seconds, I was racing down the stairs with my ears standing straight up, flicking my gaze all around. My first stop was the kitchen because that was where I had last seen him, but I came up empty.

Samuel. I heard him in my head again, weaker this time.

Yipping in frustration at my inability to help him or even locate him, I returned to the main part of the house and caught a scent I hadn't noticed in my haste through the space the first time: Dennis Keller. It was faint, but in my wolf skin my senses were sharper, so I knew it was him.

The scent originated by the front door. I leaped in that direction, realizing in midair I'd need hands to open the doorknob. I landed on two feet, turned the handle, and yanked the door open. Then I shifted back into my stronger form and dashed onto the porch.

Never before had I been able to change from wolf to man and back again so quickly and seamlessly. The power that coursed through me was stronger too. Instinctively, I knew being with my true mate was the source of those blessings. Without him, I had been a shadow, incomplete. He had changed that, changed me. And nobody would take him away. Korban was mine.

Korban! I called to him in my mind, hoping he could hear me like I had been able to hear him.

He didn't respond.

Raising my muzzle in the air, I sniffed, hoping to narrow in on his location. He had spent enough time at the house, the surrounding yard, and the adjacent woods that his scent was strong everywhere. I rumbled deep in my chest, pleased that my mate's presence was established in my den. But I couldn't relish the moment because I had to find him.

Though Korban's scent was welcome and expected, Dennis's was not. I bolted across the yard, tracking the intruder. As I neared the edge of the forest, I picked up yet another scent: Dirk Keller. Rage suffused me, my hatred for the man who killed my father rising to the surface and bubbling over. He was in my territory, threatening my mate; this time when I caught him, I wouldn't let go until he was dead.

Korban! I called out in my mind once again as I charged forward, my paws barely making contact with the dirt. I deftly avoided the trees and brush and made up Dennis and Dirk's lead. Within moments, I was near enough to hear them.

"Hurry," Dirk said.

"I'm trying, but he's heavy and it's dark," Dennis responded breathlessly.

They were carrying my mate. Korban wasn't answering my calls and they were carrying him. What had they done? Throwing my head in the air, I howled in warning and increased my speed.

"Is that Samuel Goodwin?" Dennis squeaked.

"Yes."

"He sounds close."

"That's why I told you to hurry!" Dirk snapped.

"How did he know where to track us?" Dennis sounded nervous. It was the first good instinct I'd heard the man exhibit. "You said he wouldn't know. You said he wouldn't care."

"They're not much further," Dirk said. "We can reach them."

"Did you notice that Korban smells different?" Dennis asked breathlessly. "He smells like Goodwin. Why is that, Dirk?"

He knew the answer. They both did. Even if they refused to admit it.

"There! I see them," Dirk said moments before I broke through the low-hanging branches of the final tree blocking him from my sight.

Dirk was limping.

Dennis had Korban flung over his shoulders. My mate was in his wolf form. His eyes were closed, his legs hung down limply, and the scent of his blood permeated the air.

I growled and pounced. Both men turned on their heels, their eyes wide with surprise. Dennis opened his mouth to say something, but nobody would ever know what it was because I clamped my jaws around his throat, took him to the dirt, and ripped out his jugular.

The sudden impact with the ground had my still unconscious mate groaning. I went to him, nudged his snout with mine, and swiped my tongue over his forehead, cleaning the blood clotted on top of a hot, swollen knot. When he didn't wake, I licked his lips and neck. I wanted him to open his beautiful blue eyes. I also wanted to kill every person responsible for hurting him.

Dirk hadn't stopped to help his brother, choosing instead to escape. Though he was no longer in my line of sight, I knew I could catch him with ease. Unfortunately, it would require leaving Korban vulnerable and unattended. I whined in frustration, my need to seek vengeance and eliminate the danger to my mate outweighed by my desire to protect and care for him.

Incredibly, Dirk solved my problem by returning. I scented two other males with him.

"He's over here," he said. "Goodwin's son is there too. He's in his wolf skin and he's huge, so you better shift."

If I had been able to do it in that form, I would have laughed at Dirk's stupidity. Instead, I licked Korban's neck one more time and then rose to my feet and stood over him.

Two brown wolves trotted between the trees and approached me, their lips curled, teeth bared. I didn't know who they were, but I recognized their scents. They had been two of Dirk's witnesses during the challenge against my father. I wondered how deeply the conspiracy to kill him had been.

These two shifters had followed Dirk's direction without question, come onto Yafenack land uninvited, and knowingly approached the Alpha with malicious intent. If they were willing to violate our customs and rules with such ease, I strongly suspected they'd been involved in or at least aware of Dirk's plan to poison my father. Killing them would be a joy.

Wanting to make sure I had all my targets in one place, I waited until I caught sight of Dirk, still in his human form. Then I aimed for the nearest wolf, landed on his back and buried my canines in his neck. A sharp turn of my head was all it took to snap his neck.

His death was so fast, the other wolf didn't realize it had happened until I was inches from him. He jumped, possibly trying to tackle me, but I swiped my claws at him, dug them into his belly and yanked down until his guts spilled out. With three enemies defeated, I had only one more shifter to kill.

Raising my head, I landed my gaze on Dirk Keller. He stood rooted to the ground a dozen feet away from me, his face pale, mouth hanging open, and eyes wide. I stalked him, careful to watch for any twitch of his muscles that would indicate an intent to run in a certain direction. But he didn't move, didn't speak, and looked almost like he wasn't breathing. The scent of urine hit my nose, and I saw wetness seep into his pants.

In the end, it was disappointingly anticlimactic, like killing a sheep that was too petrified to run from a predator. I jumped, landed both front legs on his chest, and pushed him to the ground. Then I buried my teeth in his throat and shook my head, sending blood splattering along the brush, trees, and soil. When all the life had seeped from his body, I released him and trotted over to my mate.

Korban was still unconscious, so I shifted into my human form, squatted next to him, and scooped him into my arms. He shifted too.

"Samuel?" he said weakly.

"Yes, it's me." I held him close to my chest as I stood. "Don't worry. Nobody will hurt you now. You're safe."

He crinkled his nose. "I smell blood." His eyes flew open, the blue gaze immediately washing peace over me. "Are you hurt?"

"It's not mine." Which was something he normally would have known based on scent alone, so the question worried me.

I dipped my face and bussed my lips over the deep purple mark on his forehead. "That bruise looks really bad. I'll get you home and then call the pack healer."

Without argument, he snuggled into my arms and tucked his head under my chin. "You were right about my father. It was exactly like you said—he was waiting for my body to be delivered so there would be no one left with a claim to be Alpha. He honestly thought the pack members would be so relieved he was healed they'd turn a blind eye to him leading the pack under his brother's name."

"And when he realized that wasn't going to happen, he came to take you?"

"He didn't want me speaking to the pack tomorrow night and exercising my claim. So he sent my uncle to your front door." Korban sighed. "I was so stupid. Dennis said he wanted to talk to me about what we told him. I invited him in, but he said he couldn't enter another Alpha's home without his permission. I didn't want to argue about the fact that he wasn't an Alpha and that, as your mate, I had every right to invite him in, so instead, I let him have his way and stepped outside to talk."

"But instead of talking, he attacked you?"

"Yes. He hit me in the head with something." He paused and knitted his eyebrows together. "A rock, I think. Everything went black, and the next thing I knew, we were in the forest and my father was there. I called for you in my head and tried to talk sense into them. When that didn't work, I shifted into my wolf, called you again, and did my best to fight him off. I think I got a few good bites on his leg, but I wasn't steady on my feet, and then Dennis hit my head again."

"They can't hurt you anymore." I curled my arms, holding him tighter. "I'm sorry I couldn't get to you sooner," I said regretfully. "You must have been so scared."

"I was a little, but I knew you'd come for me. I even told my father and my uncle I'd called for you through our mental link, but they thought I was lying." Korban raised his blue-eyed gaze to meet mine. "They refused to believe we could be true mates, and in the end, that killed them."

Though I was glad to hear his senses were still sharp enough to have identified his father's and uncle's blood, I was worried how he'd feel about their deaths and my role in them.

"I'm sorry I couldn't help," he said as he patted my chest. "Are you sure you're not hurt?"

Did that mean he understood? "I killed them," I confessed. "Dirk and Dennis both. And two other Miancarem shifters." I swallowed hard. I wouldn't say I was sorry, because that wasn't true. My only regret was that what I'd done would upset Korban. "I know they were your family, your pack, but—"

"No." He nuzzled my throat. "You're my family. Not them, not the Miancarem pack." He lifted his head and licked my lips. "You."

CHAPTER 18

WHILE THE healer examined my mate in the family room, I washed off the dirt and blood from the fight and then closed myself in the study and contacted the interpack council. Though their role in day-to-day pack dealings was normally rare, I was close to putting them on speed dial. But it couldn't be avoided.

The bodies of four Miancarem pack members, one of them the former Alpha and the other the man who claimed to be replacing him, were on my pack lands. They had come in uninvited, invaded my territory, and taken my mate against his will. I would have been well within my rights to kill them for any of those violations, let alone the lot of them. But having the right to do it didn't change the potential unrest it could cause to the Miancarem pack, especially on the tail end of all the other drama Dirk had initiated. So I called the council yet again and filled them in on what had happened.

"Alpha," Joy Griffin, the pack healer, said as she knocked on the study door.

"Come in."

She opened the door and entered the room.

"How is he?" I asked as I stood up from behind the desk.

"He's fine. He'll have that goose egg on his head for a while. It looks bad and I'm sure it hurts, but it's not serious. And he didn't sustain any other injuries."

Sighing in relief, I rubbed my palms over my face. "Thank you for coming right away. I know it's late and he told me he was fine, but I wanted to be sure."

"It wasn't a problem. I'm the pack healer—it's my job to ensure the health of our members. Please don't ever hesitate to contact me when there's a need."

I stepped around the desk and headed toward the door, eager to return to Korban's side, where I belonged. When I realized she hadn't moved, I paused and said, "Is there something else?"

"No." She shook her head. "Well, yes." She nodded. "I, uh, want to congratulate you on your mating. Even through his injuries, I could sense your mate's strength, and you seem more settled and grounded."

Joy was several years older than me, but I'd been around her often growing up because her father George had been one my father's closest friends. When Joy had come of age and announced she wanted to become a healer, something no female in our pack had done, George had sought guidance from my father. Always one to move forward rather than cling to archaic traditions, my father had sent her to train for the job, and when the previous healer retired, Joy had stepped in.

"Thank you," I said. "He makes me..." I tried to think of the right description. "I'm better with him."

She remained in place, so though I itched to get back to Korban, I waited, understanding she had more to say.

"He's male and you're male." She licked her lips nervously.

My hackles went up at the thought that she might question the veracity of my mating.

"So does that mean other pack members can do it too?"

Her tone wasn't confrontational or accusatory, which calmed my nerves, but I didn't understand what she meant. "Do what?"

Clearing her throat, she fixed her gaze on my chest rather than my eyes. "Are other pack members allowed to take mates of the same sex, or is that only because you're Alpha?"

"Oh." I blinked rapidly, processing what she'd asked. "The rules don't limit who a shifter can choose as a mate," I said. "Mating decisions are left to individual discretion."

"But the pack lore says females have to tie with males and—"

"The lore isn't the law, and besides, it's wrong." I pointed to myself. "I'm proof it's wrong."

"So you won't enforce it?"

"Enforce what?"

"The pack lore. Will you allow other pack members to choose whoever they want as a mate?"

The question angered me, not because she was asking it, but because she felt she had to. "My job as Alpha is to support the members so we can all work together to better our pack. Mating decisions are between the mates and nobody else, not even the Alpha."

"So if I want to mate with a female..." She arched her eyebrows in question as her words trailed off.

"Support the members to better the pack," I repeated. "If two females want to mate, I will support them. Having freedom to control our most personal decisions strengthens us. A pack is only as strong as its weakest member, so strong shifters make a strong pack."

Smiling gratefully, she stepped closer and wrapped her arms around me. "Thank you, Alpha."

Rather than feeling the urge to pull away, I returned the hug, warmed that my pack member trusted me with her question and her person. "You're welcome."

"Korban?" I called as I stepped into the bedroom.

"I'm here." He walked out of the bathroom, surrounded by billowy steam. "I needed to clean up before getting into bed."

He was a vision from a fantasy come to life: moonlight reflecting off alabaster skin, lean muscles working as he walked, navy eyes full of affection, and that smile.

"The first thing I loved about you was your smile," I said as I approached him.

"Is that right?" He reached for my shirt and started unbuttoning it. "I'm pretty sure you thought it was a different emotion back then."

"I was young and confused," I admitted.

He pushed my shirt off my shoulders and caressed my chest. "Two sides of the same coin."

"What?"

"Love and hate." He reached for my zipper. "They're two sides of the same coin. Both emotions are powerful, visceral. If you don't recognize one, don't expect to feel it, then you might confuse it with the other." He pushed my pants and underwear past my hips, and they pooled around my bare feet.

"I recognize it now." I cupped his cheek and traced his jawline with my thumb. "I feel it."

"I know." He turned his head and licked my palm, the action becoming increasingly familiar. "Thank you for saving me today."

"I saved both of us," I said roughly. I grabbed his hips and pushed him onto the bed beside me, then I blanketed his body with mine, covering him completely. "You're mine."

"I love belonging to you." He combed his fingers through my hair and gazed at me affectionately. "For as long as I can remember, it's all I've wanted."

I gazed at him, filling my mind and my heart with his face. "Does it hurt a lot?" I ghosted my fingertips over the bruise on his head.

"It'll heal," he said.

No matter what he endured, Korban didn't wallow in sorrow. He kept his positive attitude and moved forward.

"You're the strongest man I know," I whispered.

"Samuel?"

"Yes?"

"Make love to me?"

"Always," I said tenderly. I slanted my mouth over his, brushing our lips together over and over again.

Moaning softly, he spread his legs, leaving room for me to settle between them.

"Mmm, you feel so good." His skin was hot and soft, his cock hotter and so very hard.

"So do you." He rocked his hips up and down, rubbing himself against me. "You're amazing." He reached for my ear and nibbled on my lobe. "Can't get enough." He wrapped his legs around my backside and thrust harder. "Please, honey." He scraped his teeth over the mating mark he'd given me. "Want you."

I sat up, grabbed the bottle of lubricant we had picked up during our trip to the grocery store, and then settled between my mate's legs again, but lower down. I buried my face in his groin, groaning as I inhaled his scent. He dropped his knees apart, showing me everything.

Taking advantage of the opportunity, I began to lick all the skin I could reach—his thighs, his balls, and his dick. His symphony of moans and pleasured cries filled the room as I mouthed each of his testicles and licked the wetness of his crown. After slicking my fingers with lube, I pushed first one and then another into his hole while I sucked on his cockhead.

"Samuel! Yes," he said, bucking onto my hand. "Touch me."

After a few more pumps into his passage, I sat back on my heels, coated my dick, and then pressed it against his pucker.

He raised his head and looked at me, his lips parted, cheeks red with arousal, and nostrils flared. I held on to both of his thighs, pushed them up and out, and then I watched his face as I penetrated his body.

"God," he gasped. "Love how that feels."

When my balls were nestled against him, I wrapped his legs around me, leaned over him, and connected our lips for more kisses. He slid his tongue into my mouth, and I sucked on it as I pumped my hips, gliding my rigid cock into tight heat over and over again. Our gasps and grunts melded together like our bodies, sounds of pleasure and desire, passion and affection.

"Close," he told me.

My mating knot swelled, locking me inside him. I rolled my hips and made small motions, pushing myself against his gland on the inside while dragging my stomach muscles over his dick on the outside. Before long, Korban arched his neck and stared at me as he opened his mouth in a soundless shout and pulsed hot seed between us. The evidence of his pleasure was all I needed to push me over the edge into bliss.

"You wore me out," he said, his eyelids drooping closed.

The feeling was mutual. I rested my head on his shoulder and held him tight as I fell asleep, our bodies still tied together.

Someday, our lives would fall into a predictable pattern with no drama or violence. But that day had not yet arrived. A knock on the front door, followed by the doorbell ringing, and then another knock woke me up. I squinted at the alarm clock. It was four in the morning.

"Whoever that is, I'm going to kill them," I mumbled into my pillow.

"No. It's my turn. You got to do all the killing yesterday."

They pounded on the door again. With a growl of frustration, I threw the blanket off me, climbed out of bed, and started stomping toward the door.

"Clothes," Korban reminded me.

I grunted, got dressed in a rush, and hustled down the stairs. It couldn't have taken me more than a minute, but they'd rung the doorbell another half-dozen times in the interim. Despite their best efforts to drown themselves in liquor, I recognized the scents of the shifters waiting for me before I saw them.

Rick Collins led with his fist, swinging at me the instant I opened the door. I ducked, grabbed his wrist, twisted his arm behind his back, and pinned him to the wall. I turned my head and glared at Damon Huntsworth.

"Oh God," he said, raising his hands up and stepping back. "I didn't... I wasn't... I told him to stop. I was trying to get him back in the car." He pointed at a car parked partially in the driveway and partially in the yard. Both doors were flung open and the engine was still on.

"I know what I saw," Rick slurred. "You're lying so you can stay as Alpha, but I know what you did to the tribute."

I pulled him back and then shoved him into the wall again. "His name is Korban Keller. Use it."

"You're sick," he said. "I bet you're enjoying this right now, aren't you?"

I truly wasn't. Not even the part where I'd bested him while half-asleep and without breaking a sweat.

A car sped around the corner. It skidded to a stop in front of my house. Jason Clemson and Paul Strickland jumped out.

"Rick, stop," Jason begged. "My father told you he talked to Samuel. He told you he was fine. He's our Alpha."

"He can't be Alpha. He's a pervert." He thrust his butt back, pushing it against my groin. "Look what he's doing to me right now. I bet he's hard."

"He better not be," Korban said from behind me, amusement lacing his voice.

"Very funny," I responded.

"Who is that?" Rick asked, twisting his head to the left and then to the right.

"That's Korban, my mate. I'll let you go so you can see for yourself, but you have to calm down."

"Fine," he agreed.

I released him and stepped back. Within seconds, he turned around and jumped on me again, fists swinging.

"Rick, no!" Paul yelled.

"Damn it!" I said, avoiding his hands as I kicked his feet out from under him, sending him to the ground. I placed my foot on his chest and held him in pace. "You need to stop, Rick."

He had come to my home, repeatedly attacked me, and insulted me in front of my pack members. But I couldn't bring myself to be angry. Instead, I felt sorry for him.

With a sigh, I bent down, grabbed his arms, and helped him to his feet, keeping a tight grip on him. He wriggled and grunted, trying to get free.

"Rick," I said quietly, my voice almost a whisper. "I appreciate your concern about how you believe I treated someone. It's important for all pack members, the Alpha included, to be held accountable for their actions."

He stopped struggling and stared at me.

"And I'm glad you're brave enough to call me on a perceived injustice."

He tilted his head and looked at me suspiciously.

"But don't you think it's also important for pack members to treat each other with respect?"

Slowly he nodded.

"I'm your Alpha, but I'm also a member of this pack. You came to my home in the middle of the night. You woke up my mate. You tried to strike me." I paused and arched my eyebrows meaningfully. "Do you believe those are appropriate ways for a pack member to raise concerns?"

"No."

I let go of him and, after swaying, he stood on his own.

"Rick Collins, I'd like you to meet my mate, Korban Keller." I reached my hand out to Korban, and he took it, coming to stand beside me.

"It's good to meet you, Rick." Korban held his other hand out to Rick.

"We already met when I—"

"Sometimes we all need a chance to start over," Korban said softly. He smiled at Rick and then at Jason, Damon, and Paul. "Don't you think so?"

After that, our early morning visitors dispersed and we went back to bed. Korban slid into my arms and kissed my neck.

"I admire how you handled the pack members," he said. "My father never would have allowed people to talk back to him or question him. He would have killed Rick or banished him from the pack and beaten the rest of them."

"My father said Alphas have to balance strength and power with empathy and compassion," I said.

"Saying is easy," Korban pointed out. "Doing is much harder." He rose slightly and looked at me. "You led with your heart today and turned an enemy into a supporter. And you did it while letting him keep his dignity in front of his friends." He trembled, his eyes wet. "I am so incredibly proud to call you mate."

My mother arrived the following afternoon, and Korban instantly adored her. She asked him a million questions, doted on him, and magically cooked all his favorite dishes. My brother and sister laughed at his jokes and followed him around like he was the pied piper. Korban beamed, soaking up every ounce of familial attention.

I realized then how much I had taken for granted and how much he had missed out on, but Korban, ever empathetic, stopped me from getting morose.

"Don't feel sorry for me, honey. I don't. I won the mating lottery: a sexy, brilliant, kind Alpha, two siblings, and an amazing mother. I'm finally home."

So was I.

THE END

REVIEWS

Johnnie: I really like CC's kind of romance. It's always sweet and you can betcher ass it's gonna be sexy as hell.

— *Boy Meets Boy Reviews*

Blue Mountain: Plenty of character interaction along with the perfect blend of heart tugging moments, passion and humor.

— *Swept Away by Romance*

In Another Life & Eight Days: Perfect writing, brilliant characters and hilarious banter.

— *Two Book Pushers*

Walk With Me: This is an absolutely fabulous book

— *Wicked Reads*

The One Who Saves Me: I just love the characters from this series, the familiar feeling I get when reading all my best friends, and catching up with where they are at right now.

— *On Top Down Under Book Reviews*

Home Again: Home Again is a beautiful, well-written, love story

— *Redz World*

ABOUT THE AUTHOR

Cardeno C.—CC to friends—is a hopeless romantic who wants to add a lot of happiness and a few *awwws* into a reader's day. Writing is a nice break from real life as a corporate type and volunteer work with gay rights organizations. Cardeno's stories range from sweet to intense, contemporary to paranormal, long to short, but they always include strong relationships and walks into the happily-ever-after sunset.

Email: cardenoc@gmail.com

Website: www.cardenoc.com

Twitter: https://twitter.com/cardenoc

Facebook: http://www.facebook.com/CardenoC

Pinterest: http://www.pinterest.com/cardenoC

Blog: http://caferisque.blogspot.com

OTHER BOOKS BY CARDENO C.

AVAILABLE NOW

Wake Me Up Inside

(A Mates Story)

A powerful Alpha wolf shifter and a strong-willed human overcome traditions ingrained over generations and uncover long-buried secrets to fulfill their destiny as true mates.

Regarded as the strongest wolf shifter in generations, Alpha Zev Hassick is surprised and confused by his attraction to his best friend. His very human, very male best friend. A male shifter has to mate with a female shifter to keep his humanity, so shifters can't be gay. Yet, everything inside Zev tells him Jonah is his true mate.

Maintaining a relationship with the man he has loved since childhood isn't easy for Jonah Marvel, but he won't let distance or Zev's odd family get in their way. When unexplained ailments begin to plague Jonah, he needs to save his own life and sanity in order to have a future with Zev.

Zev and Jonah know they're destined for each other, but they must overcome traditions ingrained over generations and long-buried secrets to fulfill their destiny.

Until Forever Comes

(A Mates Story)

A sensitive wolf shifter and a vicious vampire challenge history, greed, and the very fabric of their beings in order to stay together until forever comes.

Plagued by pain and weakness all his life, Ethan Abbatt is a wolf shifter who can't shift. Hoping to find an honorable death by joining his pack mates in a vampire attack, Ethan instead learns two things: draining his blood releases his pain and his wolf, and he has a true mate - a vampire named Miguel.

Over four centuries old, strong, powerful, and vicious, Miguel Rodriguez walks through life as a shadow, without happiness or affection. When a young shifter tells Miguel they're true mates, destined to be together, Miguel sends him away. But Ethan is persistentand being together comes so naturally that Miguel can't resist for long. The challenge is keeping themselves alive so they can stay by each other's side until forever comes.

Johnnie

(A Siphon Story)

A Premier lion shifter, Hugh Landry dedicates his life to leading the Berk pride with strength and confidence. Hundreds of people depend on Hugh for safety, success, and happiness. And at over a century old, with more power than can be contained in one body, Hugh relies on a Siphon lion shifter to carry his excess force.

When the Siphon endangers himself and therefore the pride, Hugh must pay attention to the man who has been his silent shadow for a decade. What he learns surprises him, but what he feels astounds him even more.

Two lions, each born to serve, rely on one another to survive. After years by each other's side, they'll finally realize the depth of their potential, the joy in their passion, and a connection their kind has never known.

Blue Mountain

(A Pack Story)

Exiled by his pack as a teen, Omega wolf Simon Moorehead learns to bury his gentle nature in the interest of survival. When a hulking, rough-faced Alpha catches Simon on pack territory, he tries to escape what he's sure will be imminent death. But instead of killing him, the Alpha takes Simon home.

A man of action, Mitch Grant uproots his life to support his brother in leading the Blue Mountain pack. Mitch lives on the periphery, quietly protecting everyone, but always alone. A mate is a dream come true for Mitch, and he won't let little things like Simon's rejections, attacks, and insults get in their way. With patience, seduction, and genuine care, Mitch will ride out the storm while Simon slays his own ghosts and Mitch's loneliness.

All of Me

To bond with his destined mate, an Alpha wolf must look past what he sees and trust what he feels.

Bonded by their parents before they were conceived, wolf shifters Abel and Kai adored each other since they were children. As teens, the two future Alphas took the next step in their bonding process and vowed to remain true to one another until Kai came of age. But when tragedy struck, Abel felt betrayed and ran from Kai instead of completing their mating.

Abel never stops yearning for the man who was supposed to lead by his side, and after years without contact, Kai returns, broken and on death's door. If Abel wants to fulfill their destiny and merge their packs, he'll need to look past what he saw and trust his heart.

Strange Bedfellows

Can the billionaire son of a Democratic president build a family with the congressman son of a Republican senator? Forget politics, love makes strange bedfellows.

As the sole offspring of the Democratic United States president and his political operative wife, Trevor Moga was raised in an environment driven by the election cycle. During childhood, he fantasized about living in a made-for-television family, and as an adult, he rejected all things politics and built a highly successful career as far from his parents as possible.

Newly elected congressman Ford Hollingsworth is Republican royalty. The grandson of a revered governor and son of a respected senator, he was bred to value faith, family, and the goal of seeing a Hollingsworth in the White House.

When Trevor and Ford meet, sparks fly and a strong friendship is formed. But can the billionaire son of a Democratic president build a family with the congressman son of a Republican senator? Forget politics, love makes strange bedfellows.

Perfect Imperfections

Hollywood royalty Jeremy Jameson has lived a sheltered life with music as his sole focus and only friend. Before embarking on yet another international concert tour, he wanders into a bar in what he considers the middle-of-nowhere and meets a man who wins him over with his friendly smile and easy-going nature. Accountant slash bartender slash adventure-seeker Reg Moore has fun talking and drinking with The Jeremy Jameson and can't say no when the supposedly straight rock star makes him a once in a lifetime offer: keep him company on his tour by playing the part of his boyfriend.

Listening to music, traveling the world, and jumping off cliffs is fun. Falling in love is even better. But to stay with Jeremy after the stage lights dim, Reg will need to help him realize there's nothing pretend about their relationship.

McFarland's Farm

(A Hope Story)

Wealthy, attractive Lucas Reika treats life like a party, moving from bar to bar and man to man. Thumbing his nose at his restaurateur father's demand that he earn his keep, Lucas instead seduces a valued employee in the kitchen of their flagship restaurant, earning himself an ultimatum: lose access to his father's money or stay in the middle of nowhere with a man he has secretly lusted over from afar.

Quiet, hard-working Jared McFarland loves his farm on the outskirts of Hope, Arizona, but he aches to have someone to come home to at the end of the day. Jared agrees to take in his longtime crush as a favor. But when Lucas invades his heart in addition to his space, Jared has to decide how much of himself he's willing to risk and figure out if he can offer Lucas enough to keep him after his father's punishment is over.

Walk With Me

(A Home Story)

When Eli Block steps into his parents' living room and sees his childhood crush sitting on the couch, he starts a shameless campaign to seduce the young rabbi. Unfortunately, Seth Cohen barely remembers Eli and he resolutely shuts down all his advances. As a tenuous and then binding friendship forms between the two men, Eli must find a way to move past his unrequited love while still keeping his best friend in his life. Not an easy feat when the same person occupies both roles.

Professional, proper Seth is shocked by Eli's brashness, overt sexuality, and easy defiance of societal norms. But he's also drawn to the happy, funny, light-filled man. As their friendship deepens over the years, Seth watches Eli mature into a man he admires and respects. When Seth finds himself longing for what Eli had so easily offered, he has to decide whether he's willing to veer from his safe life-plan to build a future with Eli.

Made in the USA
Monee, IL
16 June 2020